HEAVEN

By David Edgecombe

CaribbeanReads Publishing, Washington DC, 20006

First Edition

Text copyright © 2016 David Edgecombe

© 2016 by CaribbeanReads Publishing

All rights reserved.

Printed in the USA

ISBN: 978-0-9964358-7-1

Library of Congress Control Number: 2016933659

For Rosalyn

Table of Contents

Preface

Goat-Mouth and Other Superstitions

In the Caribbean, to "put goat-mouth" on someone or something is to make a statement, often in jest, that turns out to be prophecy. When I said, "Frustration is the destiny of the Caribbean playwright," it was what I had already seen to be true.

Playwrights such as Errol John, the Trinidadian author of the classic play, *Moon on a Rainbow Shawl*; Derek Walcott, who would later win the Nobel Prize for Literature for his poetry; and Errol Hill, who should be named the father of Caribbean theatre; all left the Caribbean because there was no theatre here to sustain them. Some, like Hill, stopped writing plays altogether.

I once had dinner with Errol Hill and his dear wife Grace at their home in New Hampshire. He had written eight plays, including *Strictly Matrimony* and his last play, *Man Better Man,* produced in 1964. Unwittingly, I poked a finger into a wound by asking him why he had stopped writing plays.

He flinched and was quiet before saying, "I moved on to writing other things."

Grace said with fire, "The Caribbean was never kind to Errol."

Trevor Rhone was the only Caribbean playwright who made his living almost exclusively from his plays. The last time we spoke he told me he was focusing on movies. "If I could bring a movie in for under $500k," he explained, "I would be able to make the money back in Jamaica alone and would be in business." I asked about theatre and he said, "Unless you bringing filth and depravity in your plays, there's no money to be made in theatre in Jamaica today." He died in 2009.

I had worked with the Barbados-born Canadian novelist, Austin Clarke, turning two of his novels into a play called *Strong Currents* for Canada to perform at FESTAC in Nigeria. When I told him I was leaving Canada to go back to Montserrat he looked at me quizzically. He said, "Let me tell you this, David, there's no going home because they will never let you. You'll be back."

Call it self-fulfilling prophecy if you will, but I left Canada in 1977 and lasted only three years at home, albeit three productive years. I returned to work at Radio Antilles as Director of Educational Programing and was elected Artistic Director of the Montserrat Theatre Group (MTG), which I had founded in 1970. The MTG was rebuilt around a strong technical team–Winston 'Kafu' Cabey, Cyril Allen, Desmond Meade, Rolston Meade, and Willie 'Kinney' O'Garro. All actors had to audition and auditions were open to the public. A core group of actors emerged consisting of such talent as Gus White, Tyrone O'Flaherty, Elizabeth Armony, Irene Bramble, Joe West, Vereen Thomas, Althea Edwards, John Heat, and Dalton Lee. We held regular training workshops and worked hard to produce excellent theatre.

Soon we were hosting other Caribbean theatre companies: the Harambee Open Air Theatre Company of Antigua performing original plays by Dorbene O'Marde; the National Players Theatre Movement of St. Kitts-Nevis headed by Clem 'Bouncing' Williams and performing the original plays of Freddie Kissoon of Trinidad and Tobago; and the People's Action Theatre (PAT) of Dominica performing the original plays of Alwin Bully. We made several tours to Antigua, St. Kitts, St. Croix, and St. Thomas. We performed at CARIFESTA in Cuba. The monies we raised went into a fund that built a covered theatre at the UWI Centre, a project that was masterminded by Howard Fergus, its resident tutor. We were too busy, too successful. This bothered some people, including colleagues at Radio Antilles.

Then I proposed investing in ourselves by taking leave from our jobs for one year, borrowing money from the bank, and touring a play across the Caribbean. We were all young enough, I reasoned, to give a year to this venture. And who knows, maybe we would be able to prove it was possible to make a living this way or get government to fund a national theatre in much the same way as it did the radio station. Well, I must say they gave me a respectful hearing, but as soon as I was out of earshot called me 'Kerry Packer' in gleeful honor of the Australian media mogul who first offered West Indian cricketers big money for playing the game.

One actor said to me, "I doan know wey you think you going wid all this professional nonsense. All I want to do is go on stage, mek a ass o' meself, mek people laugh, an' go home, till next time." I laughed, because the only other thing was to 'bawl long water out me eye'.

I went to Cuba in 1979 as part of the technical team planning for CARIFESTA later that year. By default, I headed the Montserrat contingent to Cuba. Just before I went to Cuba, the New Jewel Movement headed by Maurice Bishop peacefully overthrew the Eric Gairy Government in Grenada. In the following year I received an invitation to attend the first anniversary of the Grenada Revolution as a guest of the new government. Christian Knaack, the German General Manager of Radio Antilles, who had travelled to Grenada to see Maurice Bishop and had been snubbed by the NJM as a 'CIA collaborator' repeatedly asked me why I had received the invitation. I hadn't a clue. He denied my leave to go to Grenada as a guest of the Revolutionary Government, and instead sent me as a journalist to cover the event. The documentary I produced garnered high praise, but I felt my days at the Big RA were numbered.

Many of the key technicians and actors of MTG were leaving to go abroad to study or live. Also, my 'Kerry Packer madness' had weakened my position in the company, allowing my detractors to get the upper hand. They said we were all working hard but were stupid to be doing so for free. And while the leader was 'getting famous,' it was at the expense of everyone else. Attendance at workshops dropped off. Support for the many production duties waned. And rehearsals, ah rehearsals, the bane of Caribbean theatre. Habitual lateness and absenteeism became even more chronic. In my eventual letter of resignation I wrote: "I would be happy to return if there were ever five people with half of my commitment willing to work together."

When I returned to Montreal in 1980, it was a necessary retreat and escape. Back at Concordia University for my Masters, I had hoped to reestablish my relationship with The Black Theatre Workshop of

Montreal (BTW) that had previously staged three of my plays, and where I had worked more diligently than at college. I pushed the BTW, or more specifically its president, my old comrade-in-arms Dr. Clarence Bayne, to mount an adaptation of my play, *Coming Home to Roost*, that had been quite a hit in the Caribbean. In Montreal it flopped.

Dennis Scott, principal of the Jamaica School of Drama who would soon leave to teach Directing at Yale School of Drama, invited me to participate in the first ever Caribbean Playwrights Conference, sponsored by Caribbean/US Theatre Exchange (CARIBUSTE) at the Reichhold Centre for the Arts, University of the Virgin Islands. It took place in January 1981 and put into workshop five new plays by five 'promising' Caribbean playwrights. They were Alwin Bully (Dominica), with *Pelee*; Ron Amoroso (Trinidad), *The Probe*; Rudy Wallace (USVI), *Philosopher Limer*; Henk Tjon (Surinam), *Stages*; and David Edgecombe, (Montserrat), *Kirnon's Kingdom*. This led to an invitation from Stage-One Productions of Barbados to produce the world premiere of Kirnon's Kingdom, directed by Dr. Michael Gilkes, professor of English at the University of the West Indies, Cave Hill campus.

Gilkes and I had a forceful disagreement when I got to Barbados. He wanted to direct a different version of the play than I envisioned. He told me it would be his version or no version. I offered to direct the play, but Cynthia Wilson, president of Stage One, said no one in Barbados knew me as a director and financial backers would withdraw support if I took over that role. I left for Montserrat to make arrangements to stage Kirnon's Kingdom there during my summer break. It had greater attendance, I believe, than any other play in Montserrat before and went on to be performed in Barbados for CARIFESTA. Years later, it was broadcast worldwide by the BBC. This success did little to end the goat-mouth I had put on myself.

By 1982 I was as bitter as Pomme Coulie. My master's program was ending and I had not a clue what to do next. While I was in this sorry state, my boyhood friend, Joel Webbe, knocked at my apartment door with an offer I could not refuse. He asked me to join him in a T-shirt manufacturing business.

Joel was then making good money with his company, W & W Electronics, an off-shore subcontractor for such Fortune 500 companies as Texas Instruments and Honeywell. Now he wanted to diversify into the garment industry with me as a partner. He seemed to have come from Heaven.

I had spent most of my life learning about and working in theatre arts with no money to show for it and with little or no understanding of business. I had come to resent this situation. A successful business of which I was part owner would give me the independence I needed to pursue theatre on my own terms. This was my opportunity.

But I had no investment money. In fact, I had no money at all, so I approached my mother for help. She said she thought I had gone to university to learn sense, not to come back home stupid. Where the hell did I expect her to get the kind of money I was talking about? Putting every guilt trip I could find to her head like a gun, I demanded that she stake me. She tried to wriggle out of it but I was relentless until eventually she mortgaged her property so I could have the money I wanted.

Webbe and I formed a company called WE Garments, Ltd. We had some success in Antigua, but never came near to reaching our goal of supplying T-shirts to the entire Caribbean. I had to research everything I needed to know and do. This was time consuming, which helped to solidify my decision to stay clear of the arts. If an idea for a play popped into my head, I sent it packing. If anybody invited me to direct or lecture or discuss theatre, I told them I was no longer in that line of work and needed all my time for my new business endeavor. Further, my mother was having recurring dreams about losing her house. For the first time in my life I knew what it was to live in fear. This put excruciating pressure on me to succeed.

I lived like this for about four years before I got a request from Dennis Parker, professor of Theatre at the University of the Virgin Islands, to produce my adaptation of Arthur Miller's *A View from the Bridge* and later, an invitation to attend its opening at the UVI Little Theatre in St. Thomas. I gladly accepted.

On my way to St. Thomas, I stopped into St. Maarten for two days and ran into my friend Roberto Arrindell of the Colebay Theatre Company on the streets of Philipsburg. He invited me to come with him to the Cultural Centre for the rehearsal of a play Colebay Theatre was taking to a festival in Aruba the very next day. He said the end of the play needed to be rewritten and he had toyed with the idea of asking me to fix it but never did. "However, seeing you right on the spot, would you come to the rehearsal and give us whatever help you could?"

I thought, 'What the hell? I was already going to see one play, what harm could it be to see another?'

As the lights came up in the theatre, I felt a stirring deep inside me. It was as if after having being long submerged in water my head had finally broken through to the surface and I couldn't get enough air into my lungs. I kept gulping as the rehearsal progressed and that initial stirring became a palpable surge of energy. This was home!

There was a problem with the play, but it was with the directing not the writing. It was not a problem I could remember seeing or reading about before, but I knew what it was. And I knew how to fix it.

We spent the rest of the rehearsal addressing it. Next morning, the company flew to Aruba where they won several awards for their production.

WE Garments came to an abrupt end soon after this. This did not faze me. I had been rudderless and afraid for those four years and was glad to see the end of that period of my life. Once again I was active in theatre with a new play, *Heaven*, churning in my head.

And yes, my mother did end up losing her house, but not because of my malfeasance. The erupting Soufrière Hills Volcano buried it around 1997, along with the rest of Plymouth.

I cannot recall the details of writing the first draft of *Heaven*, but I know the seeds for it were planted years before when some friends who were starting a new discotheque asked me to suggest a name for the joint. I said, "Call it Heaven" and they said I was crazy. Such a name would jinx the place and they would soon be out of business, they told me.

That led me to carry out a small experiment at a bar owned and operated by my old buddy John Wilson who had called my first play, *For Better For Worse*, "filthy" and nearly closed it down. I asked his patrons what they thought of the name 'Heaven' for a discotheque. The majority of men, led by Wilson, thought it was a bad idea and the majority of women saw nothing wrong with it. I was never able to figure that one out, but it got me thinking about writing a play set in a discotheque called Heaven.

The trouble was I no longer had a theatre company and wondered who I could ask to stage the play once it was written. I thought long and hard about it and called Dennis Parker one morning to tell him I would like him to look at my new play after I cleaned it up a bit. He said, "Go ahead and send it as is." I told him, "I wouldn't even send this first rough draft to my mother." He laughed and said, "Then think of me as your grandmother." I sent it to him. He called not long after to say he really liked it and wanted to stage it. He sent a list of questions and notes and I went to work.

Heaven was scheduled to premiere at UVI Little Theatre in 1990. But in 1989 Hurricane Hugo completely destroyed Montserrat and St. Croix. St. Thomas was not as badly damaged, but production of the play was postponed. Quite by chance I was at a student debate at UVI, St. Thomas, in spring 1990 when I ran into my old friend Dr. Vincent Cooper who was chair of English at the time. He asked if I would be able to come back to St. Thomas for six weeks in summer and teach a course. I came and this led to my being hired to teach English on the St. Croix Campus for the 1990-91 academic year. Heaven premiered in the spring of 1991 and I became writer-in-residence for that semester.

The members of the cast for that first performance were Neal Richardson (Wayne), Lavida Thomas (Cynthia), Norwell Donovan (Sam), Seymour Davis (Tony), and Roxanne Martin (Dilys).

I had nothing to do with rehearsals, but Dennis spoke to me regularly by phone establishing a close, collaborative relationship. He pointed out places in the script where the actors were having difficulties and made valuable suggestions for rewriting. I flew to St. Thomas for the opening and was very pleased with the hard work that had been done; and the attention paid to production details, particularly the set which was Dennis' forte.

Dennis and Dr. Rosary Harper, his UVI Theatre Division colleague and partner for many years in the Harper/Parker production team, had organized a six-day tour of the play to St. Maarten, St. Kitts, Antigua, and Montserrat. The planning and preparation were meticulous and we had great support on each island from UVI alumni.

After the St. Maarten performance, Sir Ian Valz, a Guyana-born playwright/director who had his own very active company, pulled me aside. He said he liked the simplicity of the play and the complexity it masked, but the director didn't understand the play. I told him each director brings hisher own interpretation to a work and must be allowed to do so.

He said, "That white man messed up your play."

I said, "That white man made my play possible," and pointed out that if every Caribbean playwright could have the benefit of a similar collaboration in bringing a play to life, it would serve Caribbean Theatre well.

The Heaven tour had its toughest test in Antigua. We performed in one of those narrow school halls found around the Caribbean, which was fine. What was not fine and not anticipated was the political meeting going on just a few yards away, with loudspeakers blearing, drowning out the actors. There was no air-conditioning in our hall, so the windows couldn't be closed. Dennis, Rosary, and I looked at each other wondering how could we get through this.

Then a remarkable thing happened. The audience sat at the edge of their seats and seemed to be struggling to hear every word. This went on for most of Act I and then abruptly the loud-speakers went dead. The political meeting was over. To this day I don't know if some Good Samaritan intervened on our behalf, but that is what I chose to believe happened. We still marvel at how the performance managed to survive that ordeal.

Other than that moment of tension in Antigua, the Heaven tour went off without a hitch and was a huge triumph.

Back in the Virgin Islands my collaboration with Dennis continued. I had watched every performance of the play taking notes. So too had Dennis. We met at my apartment on St. Croix for one full day to exchange notes for a final rewrite of the play. We agreed easily on almost everything except for a matter that had to do with the structure of the narrative that had arisen since the rehearsal period. I suggested a change that Dennis resisted, in fact, argued strongly against. Now, at the summing up, I told him I was 100 percent certain the change was needed and would make the play better. He didn't agree.

There were other instances like that, but none that marred the fruitfulness of the collaboration. I told him what I was saying would be clearer in the rewrite. The trouble with changing the narrative is you could never be sure if it works better until you see it on stage.

As fate would have it I was asked to conduct a theatre workshop at the Reichhold Centre on St. Thomas that summer. I agreed to do a technical theatre workshop around a production of the new Heaven. The production would have to be moved from the 100-seat Little Theatre to the 1200-seat Reichhold Centre, requiring a whole new set and lighting design. Dennis said he could direct or design, but not both. It was agreed that he would design and I would direct.

So it was that the revised Heaven got its first production. Like the first Heaven, it was exceptionally well received. Two of the original actors, Lavida Thomas (Cynthia) and Neal Richardson (Wayne) were in the second cast. They were UVI students who went on to get married causing Dennis to say it was a match made in Heaven. Jerome Kendall (Tony) and Myrenna Ogbu (Dilys) were new to the St. Thomas stage and turned out to be truly bright lights. Myrenna lit up the stage for a few years before leaving St. Thomas reportedly to tour with the remarkable Senagalese singer Baaba Maal. Jerome has matured into one of St. Thomas' most outstanding actors. Veteran actor Hans Eisler expanded his fine reputation in the role of Sam. It's to Denis' credit that he said to me after the play opened, "You called it right with that change. The play works better now."

Alwin Bully conducted an early stage reading of the play in Jamaica as one of The Company Ltd's Sunday Morning Series at Philip Sherlock Creative Arts Centre at UWI Mona. The play benefited from the feedback he sent me. I wished then and now there could be more such theatre interaction throughout the region. Instead there's little cause for encouragement in what appears to be blatant disregard for theatre. Here, on the eve of the 25th Anniversary production, at the theatre that staged the original version of *Heaven*, I received this text from one of the members of the original cast soon after he auditioned for the new production:

> Hi David,
> I auditioned for your present production Heaven. I do not know if I made the final cut. If I did, then it is with regret that I must inform you that I cannot be part of the production.
> I was excited about auditioning for Heaven because I was a member of the original cast 25 years ago. However, with that came reflections. I just realized that things have not changed in drama at the University and in the Virgin Islands as a whole I the last 25 years. I am very sorry, I cannot subject myself and family to the never changing conditions.
> Thanks for your support along the way.
> Yours truly,

Seymour Davis

I know only too well his pain and frustration. Over the past 25 years, so little has gone into the upkeep of the Little Theatre as to suggest that in the general scheme of priorities theatre is of scant significance.

***

Heaven, I was unofficially told, has since been included in the list of plays on the curriculum for the Caribbean Examination Council (CXC). This would mean it is among the plays for study in high schools across the Caribbean from Jamaica to Guyana. However, I have not received one request to produce it, or any questions of any kind about the play.

Inquiries have since revealed that once a play gets onto the CXC list, there's no clear pathway for getting it into classrooms. How could this be? And if a new play manages to make it into the classroom, then what? Are there study guides, equivalent to say CliffsNotes? Are there test banks with quizzes on the plot, characters, storyline? Are there production guides for schools that may wish to stage any of the plays? If not, who will write them? There is a huge opportunity here for scholars.

I am happy the CXC exists. We can best transcend our antiquated, debilitating education system by revamping it. And who better for this important undertaking than us? It would be tragic, however, if we get to be in charge and don't build a better education system for our children and our communities than what colonialism left us.

Central to any new education system must be the role of creativity, the imagination, the ability to confront our myriad problems and solve them. There's an important place here for theatre. It would be a burning shame if we don't use it.

Caribbean theatre has always lacked the ecosystem necessary to sustain it. It saddens me that we have not been able to build one so far. Better communication between the CXC, playwrights, scholars, entrepreneurs, ordinary people, and governments will change this. And we must not restrict our practice of theatre to the traditional understanding of the word. We must pay attention to the opportunities digital technology is providing for our children and communities to participate in theatre as never before. The National Theatre of England records the live production of plays performed in London and shows them in cinemas across England and the world. We too must find a way to do that. It would lead to more active engagement of our school children and the Caribbean community in general. It would energize playwrights and breathe new life into Caribbean Theatre.

I hesitate to predict what will happen to Caribbean theatre over the next 25 years but trust it finds a way to flower and flourish. For that matter, I do not know what will happen to Heaven in the next 25 years, but I'm not anxious. It has served me well by establishing beyond conflict the futility of my trying to escape the theatre. The lack of resources, of commitment, of progress; the pervasive, casual indifference still frustrates the hell out of me but I've made peace with that.

And hope lives on.

David

February 1, 2016

Productions

Heaven was first performed by the University of the Virgin Islands Theater at the Little Theatre, St. Thomas on April 19, 1991. It then went on tour to St. Maarten, St. Kitts, Antigua and Montserrat. The play was designed and directed by Dennis Parker. It was produced by Rosary Harper.

Following the tour *Heaven* was re-written and re-staged on August 30, 1991 at the Reichhold Center for the Arts, St. Thomas. This version of the play, which appears here with further small changes, was directed by the author and designed by Dennis Parker.

In 2016, *Heaven* is scheduled to be performed at the UVI Little Theater March 31-April 3 and April 7-9. It will then be performed at the 2nd Annual Virgin Islands' Literary Fest April 23-24.

Cast in Order of Appearance

April 19, 1991 Performance

WAYNE	Neal Richardson
CYNTHIA	Lavida Thomas
SAM	Norwell Donovan
TONY	Seymour Davis
DILYS	Roxanne Martin

August 30, 1991 Performance

WAYNE	Neal Richardson
CYNTHIA	Lavida Thomas
SAM	Hans Eisler
TONY	Jerome Kendall
DILYS	Myrenna Ogbu McGriff

March-April 2016 performance

WAYNE	Kamanza Tonge
CYNTHIA	Tamika Jude
SAM	Jerome Kendall
TONY	Paul Maynard Jr.
DILYS	Nastassia Jones

Characters

WAYNE	A schoolboy, about 17
CYNTHIA	A civil servant, 18 or 19
SAM	A businessman in his 60s
TONY	A lawyer, early 40s
DILYS	Tony' wife, 35

Setting

The annex, back yard or back patio of a discotheque called Heaven. Two round tables—one stage left, the other stage right—each with two chairs. A door leading to Heaven, up left. A door to a bathroom, right of center. Another 'exit', down left, leading to an open field or park (which does not have to be shown). The whole play takes place here, one Saturday night.

HEAVEN

By David Edgecombe

ACT I

(As the lights come up, Wayne and Cynthia are rehearsing a dance without music. They go through the sequence with Wayne counting out the steps)

WAYNE

Great! That's it! You got it! Alright, next section now. Follow me.

(He shows her some steps. She tries to follow but fails)

CYNTHIA

Man, this is too hard.

WAYNE

Easy. Let's try it again. After three. And a one and a two and a...

(They dance. She is hesitant and uncertain and misses her step)

CYNTHIA

Look, I just can't get it right.

WAYNE

Concentrate, okay, just concentrate.

CYNTHIA

It's too hard, man.

WAYNE

You almost have it. Once we run it a few more times we'll be all set.

CYNTHIA

A few more times? You no see how me tired?

WAYNE

Stop complaining and let's go from the top.

CYNTHIA

What I'm trying to tell you, Wayne, is that I can't get the steps. I don't know what I'm doing.

WAYNE

Alright. I'll show you again. Just follow me. Come on, just follow me.

CYNTHIA

(Reluctantly getting into place behind him)

Okay, Mr. Choreographer, show me.

WAYNE

Concentrate. After four. And one, two, three, four. And…

(He demonstrates and she follows)

WAYNE

How's that?

CYNTHIA

Good, so far.

WAYNE

Alright, let's try it together.

(They dance and she misses her step again)

CYNTHIA

I give up.

WAYNE

Don't. Come back and let's run through it again.

CYNTHIA

Either you come up with something simpler or let's forget it.

WAYNE

Let's try it one more time.

CYNTHIA

Let's try something simpler.

WAYNE

But this is perfect, Cynthia. It's just right. We can win with it.

CYNTHIA

But I can't get the steps right. That's what I'm trying to tell you.

WAYNE

If you had come to rehearsals you wouldn't be having this problem now.

CYNTHIA

I'm not having no problem. You're making it a problem. I say let's forget the damn contest and just enjoy ourselves tonight.

WAYNE

I asked you to dance with me, Cynthia. I asked you because I believe I could depend on you.

CYNTHIA

I thought you asked me because of my spectacular talent.

WAYNE

It's just a big joke to you, right?

CYNTHIA

No, it's killing me and that's no joke.

WAYNE

We agreed to rehearse three times. Twice you don't even show up. The third time you reach almost two hours late, and wouldn't even make an effort to get it right.

CYNTHIA

It's not that I'm not making an effort. I just didn't expect you to have something so complicated.

WAYNE

It only seem complicated because you haven't practiced.

CYNTHIA

Look, Wayne, this week was nothing but hell, so just back off, okay?

WAYNE

A lot of good dancers are in the competition tonight. We can't come with any ole stupidness and hope to win.

CYNTHIA

So let's just go in for the hell of it and have some fun.

WAYNE

I need to win!

(Pause)

I need the money.

CYNTHIA

What money? A hundred, hundred and fifty dollars?

WAYNE

A hundred each if we win. When we win.

CYNTHIA

That's money to be breaking your arse like this for?

WAYNE

Stop bitching, okay? It might not be much but it will help pay for books and school leaving exams next term. Every bit helps.

CYNTHIA

You doan need to explain it to me, Wayne. Come let's run the dance.

WAYNE

From the top?

CYNTHIA

From the top.

WAYNE

With the music?

CYNTHIA

Yeah, let's try it with the music.

5

WAYNE

Get ready.

(Wayne turns on a cassette player and they run the dance from the top. While they dance, Sam enters and watches them. At the end, he applauds)

SAM

Fantastic!

WAYNE

You like it, Mr. Drummonds?

SAM

Out of this world.

WAYNE

Looks good?

SAM

Better than good. Fabulous.

WAYNE

You see. I told you we could do it.

CYNTHIA

We haven't done it yet.

WAYNE

But, we will. Dance like that tonight and we must win the two hundred bucks.

CYNTHIA

Stop counting your chickens. What about all those good dancers competing tonight?

WAYNE

Can't touch us. Not one of them. Me and you are the best. THE BEST! Just keep telling yourself that.

SAM

Look, ley me buy you both something to drink. After that performance you must be thirsty. What you having, Wayne?

WAYNE

Coke is good.

SAM

Yeah?

WAYNE

You know, ice cold and refreshing, in bottle or can.

SAM

Oh, you had me fooled there for a minute. And you Miss... What's it again?

CYNTHIA

Corbett.

SAM

Yes, of course. What would you like?

CYNTHIA

I'll have a beer.

WAYNE

Beer?

CYNTHIA

Don't worry. I am not going to get high and forget my steps.

WAYNE

Forget the beer. Bring her a Coke or a juice, sir.

CYNTHIA

I want a beer.

WAYNE

Have your beer after the contest.

CYNTHIA

Wayne, I want a beer and I am going to have a beer. Now.

(Pause)

SAM

That settles it? Good. One Coke and one beer in a minute. I'll be right back.

(He starts to leave but turns back)

Tell you what, Wayne. You must know your way around this... Heaven better than I ever would, so why not do the honors?

WAYNE

If you like.

SAM

(Giving Wayne money from a wad of bills)

You're the one with all the youth and energy anyway.

WAYNE

A hundred dollars? You don't have anything smaller, sir?

SAM

Bigger, maybe. Smaller, no.

WAYNE

Anything for you, sir?

SAM

Brandy straight up.

WAYNE

Coming right up.

SAM

And, Wayne, make sure it's the best they have in the house. Double.

WAYNE

Nothing but the finest for you, Mr. Drummonds.

(Wayne exits)

SAM

Clearly you were born to dance.

CYNTHIA

You really like it?

SAM

Loved it. If there's a better dancer than you, she's not on earth. Or in Heaven for that matter.

CYNTHIA

I hope not in Heaven. I really want us to win tonight, for Wayne's sake. The ole jackass.

SAM

What?

CYNTHIA

Never mind me. It's just that he gets me so mad sometimes.

SAM

Don't let him get you mad. Don't let anything get you mad.

CYNTHIA

Ever?

SAM

Let's start with tonight and build from there. Tonight I don't want you to be mad. I want you to be happy.

CYNTHIA

I want to be happy too.

SAM

I want to make you happy.

CYNTHIA

Is that so?

SAM

One hundred percent so.

CYNTHIA

Why are all you men like that?

SAM

Like what?

CYNTHIA

"Forget the beer!" He's not even a man yet. Not even out of school, and he wants to pitch orders to a big woman like me.

SAM

You don't look any older than him to me.

CYNTHIA

I'm a year older. Plus he's still in school and I'm out working for my own money.

SAM

How come?

CYNTHIA

How come what?

SAM

You're out of school?

CYNTHIA

You doan know?

SAM

Haven't a clue.

CYNTHIA

Then you must be the only one.

SAM

What happened?

CYNTHIA

You don't know, you don't know.

SAM

I'd really like to know, so tell me.

CYNTHIA

No way. I'm supposed to be happy tonight, remember?

SAM

Yes, of course. Well, where were we? Oh, yes, Wayne giving you orders. Look at the bright side. Ten, maybe even five years ago you would have been happy to obey.

CYNTHIA

Me? Not me. Not ten years ago, not fifty, not ever.

SAM

It wouldn't even have occurred to you to do anything other than obey.

CYNTHIA

Never happen. Not me. Me, Cynthia Corbett? Never happen.

SAM

Hot blooded and rebellious, eh?

CYNTHIA

That's me. I'm not putting up with no crap from nobody. Not again.

SAM

Not again?

CYNTHIA

Never mind.

12

SAM

Was that your boyfriend?

CYNTHIA

What?

SAM

Wayne is your boyfriend?

CYNTHIA

It look so?

SAM

Yeah, it look so to me.

CYNTHIA

Good.

SAM

But, being a man who knows that too many things are not what they appear to be, my question still stands. Is Wayne your boyfriend?

CYNTHIA

Suppose I tell you no?

SAM

So we're going to play games, then? Alright, if you say no, is no.

CYNTHIA

And suppose I say yes?

SAM

That I'll sooner believe.

CYNTHIA

And what difference would it make?

SAM

Okay, let me put it another way: Do you have a boy-friend?

CYNTHIA

That's for me to know and for you to find out.

SAM

Oh, God!

CYNTHIA

Oh, God, what?

SAM

I thought that line was long dead and buried. I never expected to hear that one, and especially not from you.

CYNTHIA

Well, you just heard it.

SAM

And I'm very disappointed. Grossly disappointed.

CYNTHIA

That's your arse. Be disappointed all you want.

SAM

Look, forget I asked.

CYNTHIA

I'm going to look for Wayne.

SAM

He'll soon be back, I'm sure.

CYNTHIA

He's taking too long.

SAM

Relax. What's the hurry?

CYNTHIA

I want to go look for him.

SAM

Yes, of course. Please go and see what's holding up your boyfriend. Make sure no other woman is stealing him away.

CYNTHIA

Wayne just likes me, that's all. Okay?

SAM

I wouldn't hold that against him.

CYNTHIA

And I like him too. A hell of a lot.

SAM

You just don't like him giving you orders, right?

CYNTHIA

Aaah! That's nothing. I know how to deal with that. He's my best friend and I want to help him win tonight.

SAM

Good luck, although I don't see how you can lose.

CYNTHIA

What you doing here, anyway?

SAM

I want to be in the company of angels.

CYNTHIA

You don't look like a disco person to me. And, come to think of it, I don't remember ever seeing you here.

SAM

One angel in particular.

CYNTHIA

Oh?

SAM

You.

CYNTHIA

Oh, really?

(She laughs derisively)

SAM

You think it's funny?

CYNTHIA

Well, no. Not really.

SAM

So why the laugh?

CYNTHIA

Really, Mr. Drummonds. What would you be wanting with a little girl like me?

SAM

To make you happy, that's all. Ahh, I almost forgot. And to help make it possible for you to enjoy yourself, I brought you this.

(He gives her an envelope)

CYNTHIA

What is it?

SAM

Look and see. Open it. Look at it.

(Wayne enters)

CYNTHIA

Finally.

SAM

But... let's keep this between the two of us. Okay?

CYNTHIA

Alright.

SAM

Put it away and we'll speak about it later.

CYNTHIA

(To Wayne)

What took you so long?

WAYNE

You should see the crowd inside.

(Passing drinks)

Here you go, Mr. Drummonds. Here you go... partner. And here's the change.

SAM

Keep it.

WAYNE

Seriously?

SAM

Well, you worked didn't you?

WAYNE

Worked?

SAM

You went for the drinks.

WAYNE

Naah, man, that's not work. I was glad to do that for you, Mr. Drummonds.

(Wayne tries to give back the money)

SAM

Never say no to money, Wayne. Even if you think I'm a fool to give it to you, let that be my problem. Keep it. You deserve it for doing such a great job on the dance.

WAYNE

Thank you, sir. Thank you very, very much.

SAM

I used to be quite a dancer myself, you know.

WAYNE

Have any good steps you want to show me?

SAM

You bet I do.

(He does a little fancy footwork)

Twinkle-toes they used to call me. I don't get to do much of it anymore, but I still love to see good dancing. Cheers. To your success.

(They all drink)

CYNTHIA

Hey, this is not beer!

WAYNE

I said you're not to drink any beer. No beer.

CYNTHIA

I doan believe this crap.

WAYNE

Time enough for beer after we win.

CYNTHIA

Doan skylark with me, you know, Wayne. Doan skylark wid me at all.

WAYNE

Do it for me. Okay. For me.

CYNTHIA

You know what I should do for you? Take this drink and throw it over your damn head. That's what I should do for you.

WAYNE

Hey, have some respect for Mr. Drummonds.

19

CYNTHIA

Go back for me beer, Wayne, or ley me go for it me-self.

WAYNE

All joke aside, Cynthia, it will make me feel better if you don't drink. More confident.

CYNTHIA

One little beer?

WAYNE

Yeah, one little beer.

(Pause)

For me, okay? Please. Please?

CYNTHIA

I doan know why I let you manipulate me like this, you know.

CYNTHIA

(She drinks)

Coke. A big woman like me on a Saturday night in Heaven drinking Coke.

SAM

Would you prefer milk and honey?

CYNTHIA

Ugh!

SAM

You have something against milk and honey?

CYNTHIA

Never tried it and probably never will.
(She laughs)

20

SAM

Not planning to go to Heaven, then?

CYNTHIA

Doan make plans. Besides this Heaven here is the only one I intend to go to for a long, long time.

(She drinks)

Coke. I let you get away with murder, you know, Wayne Cabey, and I shouldn't.

WAYNE

(Putting his head right next to hers)

Blame it on my irresistible charm and persuasive personality.

CYNTHIA

(With mock seriousness, she threatens him with her drink)

Boy, move out me face before I dowse you with this stupid drink, eh.

WAYNE

Try.

CYNTHIA

Doan bet me, you know, Wayne.

WAYNE

Come on try.

(She feigns a couple of times)

You couldn't do it for a million dollars.

CYNTHIA

Smartass.

(She throws the drink at him. He ducks under it and grabs her from behind. Playfully he kisses her on the cheek, lifts her up, twirls her, kisses the other cheek)

Put me down! Wayne, stop it! Put me down.

(He continues to hold her. Tony enters)

Put me down.

TONY

Hey, leave the girl alone.

WAYNE

Piss off!

(To Cynthia)

Come, let's go get you back your drink.

(Wayne carries Cynthia in his arms towards the exit)

TONY
(Putting his hand on Wayne's shoulder, stopping him)

I said to leave her alone.

WAYNE
Take your paws off me, man!

(Tony applies pressure to the shoulder. Wayne screams in pain and drops Cynthia)

CYNTHIA
(To Tony)

CYNTHIA (Continued)

What you do that for?

(To Wayne)

You okay, Wayne? You alright?

(Wayne nods)

What you hurt the boy for?

TONY

Who can't hear will feel...

(To Sam)

TONY

See what the world has come to? In the olden days, you help a damsel in distress, she would hug you and kiss you and love you forever. Today, she cuss you. And you lucky if on top of that she don't turn around and kick you too.

CYNTHIA

You doan know how much I would just love to kick your arse in truth.

TONY

See?

CYNTHIA

Come on, Wayne, let's go.

(To Tony)

Bully!

(Cynthia and Wayne exit)

SAM

Hot little number, that one.

23

TONY

You telling me.

SAM

Great dancer too.

TONY

So I hear.

SAM

Hear? You're a man who's supposed to know these things.

TONY

Not anymore. I'm keeping far from these young girls, nowadays. Leaving them all to you.

SAM

Bless your kind heart.

TONY

Once upon a time women used to be in love, but not anymore. Today they all in business.

SAM

You ain't lying with that one.

TONY

Only a man like you could afford them, now.

SAM

I used to think so, but I'm not so sure anymore. The other night I took a pretty one out to dinner. First time I'm taking her out and check this. She takes one sip of her soup and says to me, you know the problem with all the younger men today? They only interested in one thing: sex.

TONY

You didn't tell her it's the problem with all the older men too?

SAM

No man. She knows sex could only be in our heads.

TONY

A bright girl.

SAM

Too bright. She tells me there's this young man has an interest in her. Always bothering her up, always wanting to take her out, always telling her if she ever has any difficulties he's there waiting and ready to help her. So she eventually agrees to go out with him and tells him about this small problem she has. Nothing serious, mark you. All she needs to make it disappear is an urgent $4,000.

TONY

$4,000?

SAM

Wait, nuh. The guy says, no problem...

TONY

That must have been you, Sam.

SAM

Hold on, man. Pretty you know, my friend. Like the morning sun. And an actress. She puts those big, innocent eyes on me and with tears in her voice says, 'No problem' he says. 'No problem, haaa! He took me home and I never saw or heard from him again'.

25

TONY

So you wrote her a check?

SAM

Almost. I swear to God she almost had me. So much so in fact that I had to see how fast I could get her home too. And I must confess she's yet to see me or hear from me since then as well.

TONY

Come on, Sam. A little $4,000 would have made her happy and she in turn might have made you happy beyond your wildest dreams.

SAM

Might have. That's the operative word, my friend, might.

TONY

You don't take a chance you can't win.

SAM

Four thousand smakeroos! And that's just for openers. Well, when the stakes get so high I leave the game up to powerful lawyers like you.

TONY

I'm out of the game long before that, man.

SAM

The big problem is though, you can't really stay out of the game. Unless you're dead, of course.

TONY

And I take it you're not dead?

SAM

Well, you never know, considering I'm in Heaven to-night.

TONY

This Heaven is not for dead people, believe me.

SAM

But then you don't get to Heaven till you rise again. So maybe there's hope. Hell, they'd better be hope in Heaven.

(Pause)

TONY

So, how's business?

SAM

As they say, a lot like sex. When it's good it's wonderful. When it's not good, it's still great.

(They both laugh)

How're things with you?

TONY

I'm thankful.

SAM

You should be, the way your cup runneth over.

TONY

You think my cup is running over, eh?

SAM

School children in Swaziland know your cup is running over.

TONY

And how come I doan know?

SAM

Don't be shy about it, my friend. Rather a cup running over any day than an empty one.

TONY

You should know.

SAM

You got that right. I've had it both ways and believe me, running over is best.

TONY

I'll drink to that. Shall we?

SAM

Definitely.

TONY

Drinks are inside.

SAM

The music inside is too loud for me. Tell you what, you run along and have your drink. I'll join you later.

TONY

Come ahead, man.

SAM

Later. I want to stay here and enjoy the fresh air a bit longer.

TONY

Alone?

SAM

As you can see.

TONY

Something tells me you're on a mission tonight.

SAM

Of course I'm on a mission. A change of pace mission... a little relaxation mission.

TONY

That's it?

SAM

What else?

TONY

Well, as you know, us lawyers don't make good believers. Something tells me you're up to more than that.

SAM

I'd love to be. I want to be. Everybody always saying how great Heaven is and now I come to see for myself not an angel to be found.

TONY

You want to see angels come inside where the action is. This is just a sort of annex, if you need some fresh air and a little more privacy. This door leads to a bathroom. Out this way, is an open field with a few benches if you need even more... fresh air.

(He laughs)

Come, let's go get a drink and see what the angels look like.

(Dilys enters)

DILYS

How you reach all the way out here already? I just turn my back for one minute and off you go leaving me all by myself.

TONY

My Darling, come say good night to a great man. And the sole reason for my apparent inattentiveness.

DILYS

Sam Drummonds? My dear cousin Sam. Well, well, well. Hi, Sam. I didn't know you went to places like this.

SAM

(Kissing her cheek)

So what am I? The devil?

DILYS

Don't forget he used to be in Heaven too.

SAM

True. And you know one of the main reasons I never came to this place before is the name?

DILYS

Heaven?

SAM

That's right. They should never have called it that.

DILYS

You're putting me on.

SAM

Dead serious.

DILYS
Did you and Tony discuss this?

SAM
Not that I remember.

DILYS
You must have.

SAM
Did we?

DILYS
He used to always say the same thing.

TONY
Great minds don't have to discuss things to come to the same conclusions.

DILYS
Tony, yes. But I never figured you for getting upset with something like this, Sam.

TONY
People have to be sensitive about such things.

SAM
Exactly.

DILYS
Oh, please, a name is just a name.

SAM
You wouldn't call your dog Jesus, would you?

31

DILYS

Why not? My dog. Or my son.

SAM

Jesus.

DILYS

That's if I can get my husband to agree, of course.

TONY

And you know I'll never agree to any such thing.

(Tony exits to bathroom)

SAM

Thank God for that.

DILYS

I know you're putting me on, Sam. You have to be. What the hell. It's just a name. Jesus, Heaven, big deal.

SAM

It's not that I'm a saint, mark you...

DILYS

Precisely.

SAM

I'm not even particularly devout. But I think certain things should always be kept sacred. Names like Jesus and Heaven.

DILYS

Oh, stop it.

(Wayne enters)

WAYNE

Please excuse me, Mr. Drummonds, did Cynthia come back out here?

SAM

Haven't seen her, son.

WAYNE

Okay, thank you.

(He crosses to the area where they rehearsed the dance)

DILYS

Let me ask this young man what he thinks. Tell me something, what you think of the name Heaven?

(Tony returns)

WAYNE

What's there to think?

DILYS

As a name for this discothèque?

WAYNE

Most appropriate.

SAM

How's that?

WAYNE

Well, it's a place where people come to be happy, isn't it?

DILYS

But of course. You're young enough to see that, but these two guys are over the hills and not with it. Maybe you could teach them something.

33

WAYNE

But it could also be hell for some people.

SAM

Is that right?

WAYNE

Well, you know... some people drink too much sometimes, or smoke up too much. Others get their girls taken away from them. Some men leave their wives at home to come in here and frolic with women half their wife's age. That I imagine must be hell for the wives.

DILYS

A most perceptive young man. What's your name?

WAYNE

Wayne. Wayne Cabey.

DILYS

You're in the competition tonight?

WAYNE

Yes.

DILYS

Then I must certainly keep an eye out for you. Good luck. And thanks.

WAYNE

Any time.

DILYS

Well, like it or not, Sam, you're in Heaven. So loosen up. Relax. Take off your tie. You'll have a better time. Come, let me fix you up.

DILYS (Continued)

(She takes off his tie. Opens the front of his shirt and breaks the shirt collar over the jacket)

There. That's better.

SAM

Whatever you say. I don't agree with you and the name, but in such matters I trust your judgment implicitly.

DILYS

Actually you chose a good night to come. We're celebrating our tenth anniversary tonight. Did Tony tell you?

SAM

Er… yes, of course. He was just dragging me inside for a celebration drink.

DILYS

Maybe we should celebrate out here instead, with all the confusion inside. Eh, darling?

TONY

Whatever makes you happy, honey.

DILYS

(To Wayne)

My husband and I are celebrating our tenth anniversary tonight. Would you have a glass of champagne with us?

WAYNE

Thanks, but I don't drink.

TONY

Tell you what, let's go inside, see if we can get my friend here hooked up with somebody and then we can all come back out later.

SAM

Sounds good to me.

(They begin to leave)

Look, you two go ahead. I'll pop in here,

(Indicates bathroom)

do what you can't do for me, and join you in a minute.

(They leave. Wayne rehearses dance movements. Sam returns from the bathroom)

SAM

Lost your dance partner, eh?

WAYNE

She'll be here, sir.

SAM

How long you worked on that dance?

WAYNE

Just tonight.

SAM

You been dancing together long?

WAYNE

All through school.

36

SAM

She's still in school?

WAYNE

No. She had to leave.

SAM

Had to leave? How come?

WAYNE

Well... er... I'm not a good person to ask, sir.

SAM

Surely, whatever it is, you can tell me.

WAYNE

I wish I could, sir.

SAM

I'm your buddy, Wayne. Talk to me.

(Pause)

WAYNE

If there's anything to tell, she'll have to tell you herself.

SAM

One of those, eh.

WAYNE

One of what?

SAM

Nothing, nothing. I can certainly understand you being loyal to her and I respect that. How much longer you have in school?

WAYNE

A few months.

SAM

And I take it you're going on to university?

WAYNE

I plan to.

SAM

To study what?

WAYNE

Medicine.

SAM

Aaaha, medicine. Good. Very good. Scholarship?

WAYNE

I hope so.

SAM

Any way you cut it, it's going to call for a lot of money. Even with a scholarship you will still need a lot of money over a long period of time.

WAYNE

I know that.

SAM

And if you do get a scholarship they'll bond you. For the rest of your life if you not careful.

SAM

And stupid politicians and flunky civil servants will treat you like they own you.

WAYNE

For a few years, maybe.

SAM

For at least the next fifteen years. A smart boy like you must be able to do better than that.

WAYNE

How?

SAM

Good question. I'll put my mind to it and come up with something. Think you might be interested?

WAYNE

Yes, sir. Very much so.

SAM

Good. I love to see smart grassroots kids get ahead. Kids with drive and determination. I always say education is the great equalizer, but the poor pay too dearly for it. Yes, I'll put my mind to it and come up with something good for you.

WAYNE

I appreciate that, sir.

SAM

Get you something else to drink?

WAYNE

No thank you, sir. I'm just going to work on the dance a bit more.

SAM

Without your partner?

WAYNE

She'll be here.

SAM

Well, make sure you knock 'em dead tonight.

WAYNE

We plan to do just that.

SAM

Catch you later.

(He exits. Wayne turns on his cassette player and is practicing his dance steps as Cynthia enters. She turns down the music)

CYNTHIA

Hi. Miss me?

WAYNE

Come ley me show you something here. Let's see if we can work it in.

CYNTHIA

No way. The dance stays as it is. Anything new at this late stage is only going to confuse me.

WAYNE

Dummy.

CYNTHIA

Dummy yourself.

WAYNE

So wha' you say happen to you all this week?

CYNTHIA

I ain't tell you? Guess not. Hardly saw you at all and you didn't even call me once.

WAYNE
I called. Left several messages at home and at work.

CYNTHIA
I would have called you back if you had a phone, but...

(Pause)

Roger called me.

WAYNE
In truth?

CYNTHIA
Four or five times, this week alone, he calling me.

WAYNE
To say what?

CYNTHIA
Not a line, as you know, Wayne, not one word, far more phone call, in two and a half years, and now, all of a sudden, he breaking me down wid calls, telling me I must pack up, resign my job and come join him.

WAYNE
And?

CYNTHIA
And? I tell him to go to hell! Two and a half years, you know, man. And he know the condition he left me in. But yet not a word, not an inquiry to see if am alive or dead or if I eat. In two and a half years! And now I must join him? No, man.

WAYNE

I agree with you, but what you mother saying?

CYNTHIA

He talk to her too, for long. She think I should go, but no way. Not me. That bastard! Anyway, let's talk about it some other time because it getting me upset. Come telling me 'bout he not taking no for an answer.

WAYNE

On another matter, Cyn. Wha' Mr. Drum...

CYNTHIA

Don't call me "Cyn!"

WAYNE

Okay, Cynthia. Wha' Mr. Drummonds give you?

CYNTHIA

What you talking 'bout?

WAYNE

When I came back with the drinks he was giving you something.

CYNTHIA

Oh God, yes. Boy, you fast, eh?

WAYNE

What was it?

CYNTHIA

None you damn business. What I did with it at all?

(She searches, finds envelope and opens it. It contains ten $20 bills)

See? 20, 40, 60, 80, 100. 20, 40, 60, 80, 200.

WAYNE

Two hundred dollars? For what?

CYNTHIA

For what? For me.

WAYNE

You goin' keep it?

CYNTHIA

De sun goin' rise tomorrow?

WAYNE

You can't keep it, Cyn.

CYNTHIA

You dotish or what? And don't call me "Cyn."

WAYNE

Cynthia! Christ, what's the matter with you?

CYNTHIA

My name is Cynthia. I don't like to be called Cyn, so don't call me Cyn.

WAYNE

All I'm saying is that I think you should give him back his money.

CYNTHIA

I didn't ask him for it, you know. I didn't beg him for no money. Is he take it on himself and give it to me.

WAYNE

All the more reason you should give it back to him.

CYNTHIA

I didn't see you giving him back the change he gave you earlier.

WAYNE

That's different altogether.

CYNTHIA

Different how? He offer you money and you keep it. He offer me money and I keeping it too. Where's the difference?

WAYNE

You know exactly where the difference is.

CYNTHIA

You know how long it take me to work for $200, boy?

WAYNE

Just give it back to him, Cynthia.

CYNTHIA

You know what I could do with this $200?

WAYNE

Regardless.

CYNTHIA

And what is $200 to a man like Sam Drummonds?

WAYNE

Why you think he give it to you?

CYNTHIA

Who the hell cares why?

WAYNE

Well, you should care.

CYNTHIA

Why the hell should I? He gee me his money, I keep it, I spent it, that's it. Fini! Kaputs! Kapeesh?

WAYNE

It's not that simple.

CYNTHIA

Couldn't be simpler. You're young, Wayne. You don't understand these things.

WAYNE

I understand this perfectly well. And you only pretending not to understand.

CYNTHIA

I understand one thing: De man gee me 200 bucks an' ah keeping it. That's all.

WAYNE

When you keep his money all you're doing is saying yes to him.

CYNTHIA

Yes to him for what?

WAYNE

Think about it.

CYNTHIA

No. You tell me.

WAYNE

You agree to sell yourself.

45

CYNTHIA

Don't be a damn arse.

WAYNE

Just think about it and you'll see what I'm saying is true.

CYNTHIA

You really believe Sam Drummonds gee me this $200 just so he could jump me body?

WAYNE

Why else?

CYNTHIA

As if I'm some ole whore?

WAYNE

In a sort of way, yes.

CYNTHIA

I want to meet the man who could buy me for $200.

WAYNE

Why would he just up and give you $200?

CYNTHIA

Because he's a nice ole man. Because he can afford to be kind. Because he likes me and wants me to be happy.

(Pause)

You don't think that's possible? You doan believe there're people in the world like that?

WAYNE

Maybe, but I don't think that's what's happening here.

CYNTHIA

Why not?

WAYNE

Because of how he looks at you when he doesn't think I'm seeing. He strips you naked with his eyes.

CYNTHIA

(In jest)

Dirty ole man.

WAYNE

That's why I'm asking you not to keep his money.

CYNTHIA

Well, Wayne, as long as it's only his eyes he's stripping me with, at $200 a strip, he can undress me as much as he likes. I'm keeping the money and I'm not even going to buy you one drink out of it.

WAYNE

Don't even talk to me until you give it back.

CYNTHIA

Don't hold your breath because I'm definitely, positively not giving it back.

WAYNE

Give him back his money, Cynthia.

CYNTHIA

I am not giving it back! Now will you just get the hell off my case and stop bugging me.

WAYNE

Sometimes you really make me sick.

(He exits)

CYNTHIA

Be sick all you want, Wayne Cabey. You could puke your guts out all over Heaven for all I care.

(Tony enters)

TONY

Oh yes?

CYNTHIA

I am not talking to you. Get lost.

TONY

Hey, I've been trying to get you alone all night and now I finally manage it, that's how you talk to me?

CYNTHIA

I'm not talking to you, man.

TONY

Hey! Come on.

CYNTHIA

You had no right to hurt Wayne like that.

TONY

Come on. He's a tough, strong boy.

CYNTHIA

No right!

(Pause)

TONY

Okay, maybe I should not have hurt him, but it's all your fault.

CYNTHIA

My fault?

TONY

Hey, come here, let me tell you how.

(She looks at him, but stands her ground. He walks slowly to her)

The mere thought of you in someone else's arms brings out the beast in me. That's all.

CYNTHIA

Oh, darling…

(They embrace and kiss passionately. Tony tries to break off)

CYNTHIA

What's the matter?

TONY

Let's go out here.

(He leads her to the open field)

CYNTHIA

(Pulling away)

Not one damn.

TONY

We're not exactly private, you know.

CYNTHIA

When you going to stop being ashamed of me?

TONY

I'm not ashamed of you.

CYNTHIA

Oh yes you are.

TONY

Really, I'm not.

CYNTHIA

So, why you pulling away from me and pulling me out into some field like I'm cattle?

TONY

I don't want the whole world poking its nose into our business.

CYNTHIA

We're all alone, Tony.

TONY

Alone in a public place? You never could tell who would be coming out here in the next minute.

CYNTHIA

I'm sick and tired of this hiding and seeking, man. I'm just not a hide and seek woman, and I'm tired telling you that.

TONY

I'll make it up to you later, okay. We'll do all the hugging and kissing and whatever else then. Okay?

CYNTHIA

Same old story every time.

TONY

Believe me, honey, I'll make it up to you like you wouldn't believe.

(Long pause)

So tell me now, what happened with you and Wayne?

CYNTHIA

What?

TONY

What were you and Wayne quarreling about?

CYNTHIA

We weren't quarreling.

TONY

So what was it then?

CYNTHIA

That's me and Wayne business.

TONY

I see.

(Pause)

CYNTHIA

Angry?

TONY

No. I'm beside myself with joy.

51

CYNTHIA

My sweet baby is angry.

(She goes to embrace him)

Oh, I forgot, I'm not supposed to touch him in public. We're barely allowed to talk to each other like two strangers.

TONY

I'm not amused, Cynthia. I'm not the least bit amused.

CYNTHIA

(Touching her pocket where she had placed the $200)

Well, my learned friend, maybe you could amuse me by telling me what a girl should do if a strange man makes her a gift of $200.

TONY

Some man gave you $200?

CYNTHIA

No, no. Not me. A friend of mine.

TONY

Which friend?

CYNTHIA

I can't tell you that.

TONY

Why not?

CYNTHIA

She told me in confidence.

TONY

Who is it?

CYNTHIA

I don't want to tell you.

TONY

Well, I want to know, so tell me.

CYNTHIA

Look, just forget I mentioned it. Okay?

TONY

So, some strange man gave your—mysterious friend $200?

CYNTHIA

I said let's…

TONY

Is that what you're telling me?

CYNTHIA

That's right.

TONY

Out of the clear blue sky?

CYNTHIA

Well, not exactly out of the clear blue sky. He met her yesterday and gave her an envelope with a card. The card said, "I think of you often" and in it was $200.

TONY

That's it?

CYNTHIA

That's it.

TONY

Can't be more out of the clear blue sky than that.

CYNTHIA

So she asked me what I think she should do. I told her she should spend the damn money. What you think?

TONY

Well, it depends.

CYNTHIA

Answered like a true lawyer. Depends on what?

TONY

Whether or not the girl is willing to sell what the guy is looking to buy.

CYNTHIA

What's all this crap about buying and selling?

TONY

Manna doesn't exactly fall from Heaven anymore, you know. A guy puts out that kind of bread, he's looking for goods and/or services in return.

CYNTHIA

What if the guy is her uncle or father?

TONY

Well, is he?

CYNTHIA

No, but maybe he just wants to be nice to her. And even if he is looking for something in return, what's to stop her from spending his money and not delivering.

TONY

She could get away with that once, twice, maybe even three times. But if she wants to keep him putting out, she's going to have to start putting out too.

CYNTHIA

I don't agree.

TONY

It doesn't matter if you agree or not. It's a law of life, like gravity.

CYNTHIA

One shot. She takes his money and run and that's it. What could he do her?

TONY

Absolutely nothing.

CYNTHIA

As a matter of fact, if he keeps giving her money, as long as she doesn't ask him for it, she could take it, do what she wants with it and never give him a thing in return.

TONY

He's never going to keep giving indefinitely… unless he's getting something in return.

CYNTHIA

So he stops giving, she stops taking. No big deal.

TONY

Only that by now she's hooked. All that easy money. She needs to keep it flowing in.

CYNTHIA

Doesn't have to be. She takes his money till he comes to his senses and stops giving. And she doesn't give him one damn thing in return.

TONY

But chances are she will want a new outfit to wear to Heaven. And a new hairdo. Maybe it's the end of the month, so she has bills to pay. She has to get some groceries. There are a hundred good reasons why she needs that money. And once she keeps taking it, sooner or later she too is going to have to put out. So, if she doesn't want to get trapped, the best thing is not to take his money in the first place.

CYNTHIA

That's the same foolish talk I was getting from Wayne.

TONY

You discussed this with Wayne?

CYNTHIA

Sure, I discussed it with him.

TONY

Is there anything you don't discuss with him?

CYNTHIA

Please, don't start that again.

TONY

I would really like to know the truth about what's going on between the two of you.

CYNTHIA

For the last and final time, Wayne is my friend. You don't expect me to have any friends?

TONY

The final result of any friendship between a man and a woman is sex.

CYNTHIA

Says who?

TONY

I'm telling you that. Let them deny it all they want. Let them avoid it all they want. Let them run away from it. Once the friendship continues, sooner or later, they're going to end up in bed.

CYNTHIA

Well, I don't believe that.

TONY

You don't have to believe the earth is round either.

CYNTHIA

Look, why don't we go dance or something?

TONY

What's the 'or something?'

CYNTHIA

You really want to hear?

TONY

Sure I want to hear. Tell me.

(Dilys enters)

DILYS

There you go disappearing on me again. Come, let's dance. Your favorite song is playing.

CYNTHIA

He's talking to me. Can't you see?

DILYS

Excuse me, and who are you?

CYNTHIA

That's for me to know and for you to find out.

DILYS

Well, you can rest assured that I haven't the slightest interest in finding out. However, this man here happens to be my husband and if you don't mind I'd like to dance with him now. Come on, Tony, let's go.

TONY

(To Cynthia)

Look, the best place for us to discuss that title deed is really my office. So, why don't you drop in and see me early next week?

CYNTHIA

Man!—Just go 'bout you business, eh.

DILYS

Title Deed?

TONY

You know how it is, darling. Even in the discothèque people always want to talk business with me.

(They exit)

CYNTHIA

Hell!

(Sam enters)

SAM

What's my favorite dancer doing out here all by her pretty self? Tell you what, why don't we leave? You could come to my house, listen to records, sip as much wine or beer as you like, swim in my pool, sleep, and, tomorrow, I'll serve you breakfast in bed. How about it?

CYNTHIA

No thank you.

SAM

We can skip the breakfast in bed part if you have to leave before tomorrow. Or if you prefer, I can take you straight to your home.

CYNTHIA

I'm not ready to go home.

SAM

Then let's just go somewhere else.

CYNTHIA

I'm staying right here.

SAM

The night is not going to get any better for you here, you know.

CYNTHIA

What you mean?

SAM

You know what I mean.

CYNTHIA

No, I don't.

SAM

You happy with your little gift?

CYNTHIA

Your $200?

SAM

Your $200.

CYNTHIA

You want it back?

SAM

Of course not.

CYNTHIA

Nobody is going to buy me for $200.

SAM

You, for $200? That couldn't even pay for the dirt under your fingernails. Look, Cynthia, let me explain what's happening here. When I spotted you along the road earlier this evening, looking a ride into town, I couldn't believe my good fortune. And let me say here, if you were my woman, you would never have to stand by the side of any road looking for any ride any place. I would treat you like a queen, as you ought to be treated.

CYNTHIA

You don't even know me.

SAM

True. In fact, before tonight I could only remember seeing you two or three times. But each time I got this feeling I should get to know you better. So, when you came into the car, I was determined to talk to you, but you wouldn't let me make any headway, so I said forget it. Only I couldn't forget it. After I dropped you off, I couldn't get you off my mind. I went home and went to bed but you were still right there in the room with me. I tried closing my eyes but your face was painted onto my eyelids. So I got dressed and came back here to look for you. Now, I am not a man of many fancy words and I don't like beating around the bush, so let me put my cards straight on the table. I want to take you home tonight. And I want you to give us a chance to get to know each other better. And then, I want you to give me the chance, the opportunity, the privilege to take care of you in the grand style you deserve.

CYNTHIA

Well, supposed you were a man of many fancy words? You'd talk life right back into the dead.

SAM

Is that supposed to be a compliment?

CYNTHIA

I'm not sure. You sound too much like a politician.

SAM

Ah, but there is a difference. For the most part they're just full of ole talk. When you get to know me better you'll find out that I have both the capability and the capacity to deliver what I promise.

CYNTHIA

IF I get to know you better, you mean.

SAM

No, my dear, WHEN.

CYNTHIA

Don't be so flipping cock-sure with me, buster.

(Tony enters)

TONY

Am I interrupting something?

SAM

Not at all.

TONY

Let me talk to you a minute, Sam.

SAM

(Moving towards Tony)

Shoot.

TONY

Do me a favor would you?

SAM

If I can, sure.

TONY

Go dance with Dilys and keep her busy for me for a bit. Okay?

SAM

Sure. No problem at all.

(Sam exits)

TONY

What was that old fart saying to you?

CYNTHIA

You have a hell of a nerve.

TONY

I'm not joking, Cynthia.

CYNTHIA

Get lost.

TONY

What did Sam Drummonds say to you?

CYNTHIA

What did your wife say to you?

TONY

Look, leave Dilys out of this.

CYNTHIA

What did your frigging wife say to you, Tony Thompson? What did she say to you? Until you can answer me that don't come asking me no shit.

(He makes to slap her)

Hit me! Yes go ahead and hit me, if is trouble you looking for.

TONY

(Bringing his hand to her cheek without slapping her, he fondles it roughly)

A fine cheek. A lovely, delicate jaw. Try never to give me cause to break it.

63

CYNTHIA

Tonight was supposed to be my night. Our night together. We planned it, Tony.

TONY

I know, but would you please try to be understanding?

CYNTHIA

I'm tired of trying to be understanding.

TONY

I completely forgot today was my anniversary. I couldn't very well say to Dilys I wasn't taking her out tonight.

CYNTHIA

How charming. Well, what about Cynthia? What about giving Cynthia a little understanding for a change?

TONY

Oh, come on... .

CYNTHIA

Don't 'oh-come-on' me. You should have let me know our date was off so I didn't have to come down here like this for you and your wife to make an arse out of me.

TONY

Listen, I will take Dilys home early and come back for you so we can still spend some time together tonight.

CYNTHIA

Don't bother.

TONY

What you mean don't bother?

CYNTHIA

Just that. Someone else is already taking me home. So you can go home and stay home with your fat wife.

TONY

Quit fooling around, Cynthia.

CYNTHIA

You think I'm fooling around eh! Well I'll have you to know I'm dead serious.

TONY

You better not be.

CYNTHIA

Watch and see.

TONY

Who's taking you home?

CYNTHIA

None of your damn business, buster.

TONY

Why do I waste my breath asking? I'm the only person taking you home tonight.

CYNTHIA

Don't be so sure. I'm tired of this second string you're making me play. I want to go home first class tonight. And you know what my admirer said? He said if I was his woman I wouldn't have to stand by the roadside begging any ride again—ever. He said he might even buy me my own car.

TONY

Sam Drummonds! That has to be Sam Drummonds, right?

CYNTHIA

And so what if it is?

TONY

And did he also invite you to his house to listen to music and sip wine, spend the night and have breakfast in bed?

CYNTHIA

How you know that?

TONY

It's his standard pitch, for god's sake. Only a sucker could fall for that bucket of crap.

CYNTHIA

He also invited me to swim in his pool.

TONY

Oh yes, I forgot that. Swim in his pool.

(He laughs)

Swim in his pool.

CYNTHIA

But does he have a pool?

TONY

Sure he does.

CYNTHIA

And does he have a stereo that plays music? And is his wine good?

CYNTHIA (Continued)

And is he able to put a woman up overnight and give her breakfast in bed the next morning?

TONY

All of that is beside the point.

CYNTHIA

All of that is the point. If it exists, if it is real, if it is possible, if he can do what he says, how can it be crap? And considering my situation, what do I have to lose by accepting his invitation?

TONY

Cynthia, I want you to listen to me very carefully. And I want you to note that I'm not smiling, I'm not laughing and I'm definitely not joking. Under no circumstances are you to let Sam Drummonds take you home tonight.

CYNTHIA

Ha, ha, ha!

TONY

I don't want him taking you home. I don't want him anywhere near you.

CYNTHIA

Come to think of it he's not a bad looking guy. A little old maybe, but not at all bad.

TONY

Sam is not a man to fool with.

CYNTHIA

I'm sure.

TONY

I'm not joking, Cynthia, I don't want you messing with him.

CYNTHIA

I'm sick and tired of you messing with me, Tony Thompson. Messing up my whole life. You can't understand that?

TONY

You think I'm messing up your life? You want to see what it's like for your life to be messed up, get involved with Sam.

CYNTHIA

I'm not listening to you.

(She crosses towards open field)

TONY

Try and remember Roger McPherson.

CYNTHIA

I don't have to try.

TONY

Think about him all the time, eh?

CYNTHIA

What the hell you expect?

TONY

You know what his relationship was with Sam?

CYNTHIA

He didn't even know Sam.

TONY

So you think.

CYNTHIA

What was his relationship with Sam?

(She crosses back to Tony)

TONY

I'm not sure you want to know.

CYNTHIA

Well, I'm sure I want to know, so tell me.

TONY

Under one condition.

CYNTHIA

And that is?

TONY

That you don't let Sam take you home.

CYNTHIA

Well, if you feel so strong about it, what can I say? I supposed you'll make arrangements for a taxi to take me home.

TONY

I'm taking you home. I told you that already.

CYNTHIA

Yes, of course, I forgot. So what was between Roger and Sam?

TONY

You know what business Sam is in?

69

CYNTHIA

He has some kind of gift shop, I think.

TONY

And what kind of shop is going to give him the kind of life-style he has?

(Pause)

His real business is drugs.

CYNTHIA

He… he… was in it with Roger?

TONY

He cultivated Roger because Roger was a pharmacist and could legally help him with his illegal business. It was he who got Roger involved in the first place and Roger served him well for many months. But when the Drug Enforcement Administration in the States tipped off the police here, Sam was also tipped off. So he arranged to walk away from it completely and let Roger take the heat.

CYNTHIA

So that's who it was, Sam Drummonds? Sam Drummonds is that awful sonofabitch?

TONY

And he's always on the lookout for new talent. Anybody he can use. Which is why I don't want you getting close to him.

CYNTHIA

Look how he hurt Roger, man. Look how he hurt me. You can't imagine how many times I said in my heart if I only find out who the bastard is I would kill him.

TONY

It was also he who gave you that $200, right?

CYNTHIA

What $200?

TONY

The one you told me about earlier.

CYNTHIA

I told you somebody gave me $200?

TONY

Well…

CYNTHIA

Well? Well? Don't try pulling any fast ones like that, Tony, because it's not going to work. I told you the money was given to a friend of mine. Why you can't believe me and let it rest?

TONY

You know the answer to that already.

CYNTHIA

Yes, I know.

CYNTHIA AND TONY

Us lawyers don't make good believers.

TONY

And you know why?

CYNTHIA

I have a reasonably good idea, but tell me.

TONY

Because our business is the underbelly of the beast, so we get to see, every single day, what a truly shitful world this is.

CYNTHIA

I love you Tony, I really do, but sometimes this relationship makes me more miserable than I ever want to be.

TONY

It will get better, believe me.

(Wayne enters)

WAYNE

It's time to get ready for the contest.

CYNTHIA

I almost forgot about that. I hope I haven't forgotten the steps. Check you later, Tony, got to get dressed.

(She kisses him on the cheeks and exists)

TONY

Wayne, hold on a minute.

WAYNE

What?

TONY

Caught you off guard earlier with that hold, eh?

WAYNE

Man just leave me alone, okay.

TONY

Come on, it's a useful grip for any tae-kwon-do man to learn. I'll show it to you.

WAYNE

No thanks.

TONY

I'm not going to hurt you, man. How's the shoulder now?

WAYNE

I'm in a hurry.

TONY

Look here, give it to me a minute. Relax. It will make the arm feel better. Stronger.

(He massages Wayne's shoulder)

Okay, move it up and down, backwards and forwards. Move the whole arm around now. Up, two, three, four. And back, two, three, four. How's that?

WAYNE

Same as before.

TONY

Well, let's hope it doesn't kill you.

(Wayne starts to leave)

And by the way, Wayne, I admire the position you took regarding the $200.

WAYNE

What $200?

TONY

You know.

WAYNE

I don't know.

TONY

Sure you do.

WAYNE

I don't know what you're talking about.

TONY

The $200 Mr. Drummonds gave to Cynthia.

WAYNE

Oh.

TONY

I agree with you one hundred percent. She ought to give it back.

WAYNE

I told you, I don't know what you're talking about.

TONY

She told me all about it. What you said to her makes a lot of good sense.

WAYNE

I still don't know what you're talking about.

TONY

That's how you plan to play the game?

WAYNE

What game?

TONY

My mistake. Forget I mentioned it.

(Tony turns away and Wayne again moves towards the exit before looking back)

WAYNE

Tony!

TONY

Yeah?

WAYNE

Piss off!

(Wayne exits. Sam and Dilys enter)

DILYS

What's the big attraction out here?

TONY

What you talking about?

DILYS

You're spending more time out here than dancing in the disco.

TONY

I don't like it when it's over-crowded.

DILYS

You're not going to watch the contest?

TONY

No. I don't think so.

DILYS

What about you, Sam?

SAM

I'm going to keep Tony company.

DILYS

Look at the two of you. Two spoil sports. I came out to enjoy myself and that's exactly what I'm going to do. See you guys later.

(Dilys exits)

SAM

Everything under control?

TONY

No tears.

SAM

As yet.

TONY

What's that supposed to mean?

SAM

Just a joke, my friend, just a joke.

TONY

Oh.

SAM

This is Heaven, man. There's not supposed to be any tears here—ever.

(Pause)

Wouldn't it be wonderful to live in a world without tears? Or even to have the assurance that after death we'd go to a place where there's no tears?

TONY

What the hell are you talking about?

SAM

Ahhhhh! Just that it's curious about heaven, when you think about it.

TONY

If you think about it.

SAM

When you think about it. And at my age you get to thinking about it more and more.

TONY

How old are you, Sam?

SAM

A lot older than you, my friend. Old enough to start seriously pondering these things. Death, heaven, hell. Redemption, salvation. How did jealousy get into heaven? Ever think of that? How did it manage to find its way into Lucifer's heart? And he went with one third of the angels, you know, Tony. A whopping 33.3%.

TONY

In an election you'd consider that a good showing, eh?

SAM

Exactly. Precisely. Good enough to encourage anybody to try again. Which brings me to the heart of the matter. When all is said and done, when Christ comes again and sets up his kingdom, what guarantees do we have that in that New Jerusalem, that perfect Heaven, Lucifer will not find a way to try again?

TONY

Look, what we getting into all this heavy crap for?

SAM

Answer the question.

TONY

Well, according to my Bible, Lucifer will be bound hand and foot and cast into an everlasting lake of fire.

SAM

Ah! But who's to say that some new Lucifer or Tony or Sam, will not look across his avenue of gold to his brother's house and think: he got a nicer mansion than me. His view is better. Pretty soon this ungrateful malcontent begins to agitate, begins to stir up trouble. And this time around he might be more effective than the first Lucifer. He might be able to swing 55 or 60%. What then? What would that make of all our pain and anguish and sacrifices?

TONY

You had too much to drink, Sam. That's the liquor talking. You should go home and sleep.

SAM

I'm at least as sober as you. If not more so.

TONY

Well, I never joke about things like heaven. That's God's domain and I don't skylark with God. What I do know is that on earth you must be eternally on guard against treachery.

SAM

Yes?

TONY

Treachery!

(Slamming his hand on table)

How the hell you could be taking up $200 and giving it to my woman to come to your house for wine and music and breakfast?

SAM

How was I to know she's your woman?

TONY

Everybody knows she's my woman.

SAM

Including Dilys?

TONY

Dilys is not concerned with this.

SAM

Oh, really?

TONY

Of course, if you want to waste your money, don't let me stop you.

SAM

Seriously, I didn't know she was your woman. I thought your only woman was Dilys.

TONY

Oh, come on.

SAM

Seriously, I thought your only woman was your wife and others are just... well... pussy.

TONY

I never think of a woman as being 'just pussy'.

SAM

Of course.

TONY

I'm serious.

SAM

Sure you are.

TONY

You think I'm joking but I'm very serious. I have more respect for women than that.

SAM

Naturally, Tony. I'm ashamed of myself for thinking otherwise.

(Sam laughs)

TONY

You think it's funny, eh?

SAM

It's the most serious thing I've heard all night.

TONY

Well, there's something not so funny I've been meaning to talk to you about for some time.

SAM

Talk.

TONY

You're far too careless with your money, too conspicuous. You're drawing attention to yourself and that's not smart.

SAM

Is that a fact?

TONY

A fact, or a joke. It's up to you.

SAM

It wouldn't be a threat by any chance?

TONY

Just good advice from your lawyer. But you may laugh at it if you like.

SAM

When my lawyer offers me free advice, that is serious. Or do you plan to invoice me later?

TONY

I'm really not joking, Sam. You have a good cover for your—operation, but think of it. Who's going to believe your gift shop can generate the kind of dollars needed to support your life-style? Of course it doesn't matter too much here because nobody really gives a damn one way or another about anything, but America has declared a world war on drugs and they have people sniffing around everywhere. It wouldn't hurt to be more cautious.

SAM

You're right, but don't forget your own operation.

TONY

I'm a lawyer.

SAM

Of course, and that has to be the perfect cover.

TONY

I also happen to be 100% legitimate.

SAM

Perhaps. But some of those characters I see you doing business with, are some of my best clients.

TONY

What does that have to do with me?

SAM

Think. How legitimate can they be? You don't have to be any genius to know that this 'off-shore' bank business you and them are wrapped up in is mostly scam.

TONY

I'm not involved in any scam. I provide a legal service and collect my fees, that's all.

SAM

You're missing the point.

TONY

You don't have a point.

SAM

The point is, our world is not perfect and we both profit from this simple fact.

TONY

What the hell you saying? You comparing my legitimate legal practice as a barrister and a solicitor with your goddam drug peddling operation?

SAM

It feeds me and it feeds you.

TONY

It most assuredly does not feed me!

SAM

You may not wish to think so...

TONY

It doesn't frigging feed me, man!

SAM

Okay, okay. Whatever you say. But you should keep this in mind. If today, by any set of circumstances, the FBI, let's say, starts to poke its nose into my business get ready for them poking their nose into yours by tomorrow.

TONY

You threatening me, Sam?

SAM

Damn right I'm threatening you!

TONY

Well, let them come. Let them come and start to poke. Better yet, let's bring them. Let's call the police now. Let's call the FBI, the DEA, the CIA and all if you like. Let's invite them to come take a look at our affairs.

SAM

Tony, Tony, my buddy, let's not be rash. Let's not lose our grip on things because of some silly twit of a girl...

TONY

I don't regard her as a silly twit.

SAM

Whatever.

TONY

She's my woman. And to be frank with you, I don't like people messing with my woman.

SAM

You will risk everything for this woman?

TONY

You're the one with something to risk, Sam, not me.

(A burst of excitement comes through from inside)

SAM

Seems to me this wonderful woman of yours is inside having a ball with another man.

TONY

Wayne? Wayne is just a young punk.

SAM

And me?

TONY

You know what you are, you know who you are.

SAM

Maybe you're taking Wayne too lightly. Maybe he'll dance away with first prize and with your woman as his bonus prize. What then?

TONY

I already said all I have to say.

(More excitement from inside)

SAM

Sounds like they're having a wild time in there.

(Pause)

SAM

Sure you don't want to go check it out, make sure everything is—copacetic?

TONY

Quite sure.

SAM

Well, my buddy, look at it this way, you're in great company.

TONY

What company?

SAM

God is also jealous.

(He laughs. Cynthia and Wayne enter. She is in very high spirits, singing and dancing)

CYNTHIA

Oh my goodness gracious, weren't we smashing? Weren't we fantastic? Weren't we just out of this world?

TONY

You're always fantastic.

CYNTHIA

Well, weren't we? Now wait a minute, you didn't see our performance did you? You good for nothing so and so. How could you? Well, you missed the show of your life.

SAM

How about a repeat performance?

CYNTHIA

Not on your life.

SAM

Come on, show us your stuff.

CYNTHIA

No way.

TONY

That's a great idea.

CYNTHIA

Forget it. You should have gotten up off your arse and come see us knock everybody dead. Too late now.

SAM

Did you win?

CYNTHIA

Don't ask me any question, you bastard?

SAM

Hey... ?

TONY

Cynthia. Please.

CYNTHIA

I don't want him saying anything to me. Ask him to have nothing to do with me.

SAM

Now, wait a minute... .

CYNTHIA

I'm serious, Tony. Ask this scum-bag to keep as far away from me as possible. Come on Wayne, let's go change.

(She starts to exit and comes face to face with Dilys who is on her way to the bathroom. They exchange looks and Dilys exits)

On second thought, let's do our dance out here.

WAYNE

What?

CYNTHIA

You heard. Let's show our stuff.

WAYNE

You're crazy.

CYNTHIA

I'm serious.

WAYNE

You can't be. Forget it.

CYNTHIA

Let's do it, Wayne.

WAYNE

I'm not going to dance for those two guys.

CYNTHIA

Then dance for me. I danced for you inside. Now I'm asking you to dance for me out here.

WAYNE

Really, Cynthia...

CYNTHIA

Come on.

(She drags him to the dance area)

Start the music.

(He does and they dance with great confidence and passion. Dilys comes out of bathroom and stands upstage watching. When the dance ends both men clap wildly)

CYNTHIA

Thank you so much folks. We're glad you loved us. If you want you may leave a token of your appreciation in the hat at the door. But right now our fans are waiting so we must be off. Let's go, partner.

(She drags Wayne with her and speaks directly to Dilys)

Don't call us. We'll call you.

(Cynthia and Wayne exit)

DILYS

Really now, who is that girl?

BLACK OUT

ACT II

(Same as Act One. No time has elapsed. The action continues from exactly where it stopped at the end of Act One)

DILYS

Gentlemen, I asked you a question. Who was that girl?

TONY

Her name is Cynthia Corbett. Now, if you don't mind, let's all go inside and have some more champagne.

DILYS

Who is she?

TONY

I just told you.

DILYS

What does she do?

TONY

She's a civil servant, I think.

DILYS

You think. And one of your clients?

TONY

Yes. She's one of my clients.

89

                    DILYS
How come she was dancing for you?

                    SAM
I asked her to, Dilys. That was my doing.

                    DILYS
And of course she was only too happy to oblige. I
wonder why?

                    SAM
She loves to dance.

                    DILYS
Sam, let Tony answer me.

                    TONY
Hey, why the cross-examination?

(Pause)

                    DILYS
Just that she's so—pretty. You don't find her pretty?

                    TONY
She's okay.

                    DILYS
That's all? Just okay?

                    TONY
Sure she's pretty, but so are you.

                    DILYS
Not like her.

                    TONY
In my eyes you're the prettiest woman in the whole
wide world.

DILYS

Maybe I'm getting a little too old for you.

TONY

You're my queen and my angel. Don't ever lose sight
of that. My queen and my angel. Always.

DILYS

So pretty. And so young. So—fresh.

TONY

Forget about her, sweetheart. Believe me, she's nothing to me. Absolutely nothing. So put her out of your
mind and let's enjoy ourselves.

DILYS

A client.

TONY

A client! That's all.

DILYS

Well, I don't believe you.

TONY

What!

DILYS

I said I don't believe you.

TONY

You don't believe me?

DILYS

Yes. I don't believe you one little bit!

91

TONY

You gone crazy?

DILYS

Something is going on between you and that girl and I want to know what it is.

TONY

You definitely gone off your mind. You gone clean off you fu… cotton-picking mind!

SAM

Hey, Tony…

TONY

Stay out of this, Sam. Look, woman, who the hell you think you talking to like that? How dare you even think of…

SAM

Tony! What you getting steamed up about? Relax, man. Don't spoil her night. Let it pass.

(Pause)

TONY

Look, if you lost your senses, try and find them quick. When you do, I'm inside.

(He storms out)

DILYS

He has such a nasty temper. Thanks.

SAM

No need to thank me.

DILYS

You must forgive me, cous'. I'm not usually like this.

SAM

Maybe you need to stand up to him more often.

DILYS

Must be the drink. Maybe I've had too much to drink.

SAM

Really, you should consider standing up to him a bit more.

DILYS

This jealous wife bit is not becoming. Not becoming at all. And definitely not me.

SAM

You heard what I said?

DILYS

You saw how he got on just now?

SAM

Stop allowing him to intimidate you.

DILYS

How come you're telling me this? How come you're not taking up for him as usual?

SAM

I don't like what I just saw.

DILYS

You've seen it before, and it never bothered you before, so why is it bothering you now?

93

SAM

You're perfectly right, if it doesn't bother you, why should I let it bother me?

DILYS

I stand up to him, you know, Sam, but in matters of importance. Just now I went too far over stupidness.

SAM

Whatever makes you happy.

DILYS

I'll go look for him.

SAM

He expects you to come running after him. Don't. Leave him alone. Let him come to his senses and he'll be running back to look for you soon enough.

(Wayne enters)

Any word from the judges?

WAYNE

Not yet.

(Pointing to the cassette player)

I forgot this.

SAM

I've been keeping an eye on it for you.

WAYNE

Thanks.

DILYS

I really must go look for him, Sam. Excuse me.

(She exits)

SAM

Where's your dance partner?

WAYNE

With your friend, Tony, if you must know.

SAM

You don't like that, do you?

WAYNE

Do you?

SAM

Maybe his wife will catch him red-handed.

WAYNE

What good will that do?

SAM

You might be surprised. She may take him home and keep him home. Leave the course clear—for you.

WAYNE

Wouldn't make any difference to me.

SAM

A most attractive girl this, Cynthia. Hell, a stunning girl. But you mustn't let her steal your heart. Eh, ole buddy?

WAYNE

Why you say that?

SAM

Because, more than likely, she would break it. Probably caused you untold pain already, right? Right, ole buddy?

WAYNE

Well.... .

SAM

You have to protect yourself from women like her, Wayne. 'Cause if you not careful, she will cause you even more pain. And pain, woman pain, can wreck even the strongest man.

WAYNE

She and I are just good friends, okay?

SAM

Just good friends?

WAYNE

That's right.

SAM

Good. I'm happy to hear that.

WAYNE

Why?

SAM

One of the most profitable lessons a young man can learn is how to handle women. And you know what the key to handling them is? Understanding them. And the only way you could understand them is not to get emotionally tied up with them. You understand?

WAYNE

Yes, sir.

SAM

You think you understand Cynthia?

WAYNE

Sometimes. But really, sir, I prefer not to discuss her.

SAM

You think you know her well?

WAYNE

As well as can be expected.

SAM

What would you say if I told you I'm going to take her home with me tonight?

WAYNE

You?

SAM

That's right.

WAYNE

To your house?

SAM

All the way home to my house.

WAYNE

No way. No possible way!

SAM

Look and learn.

WAYNE

There's no way on earth, Cynthia will do that.

SAM

I'm glad you think so.

WAYNE

I know her, Mr. Drummonds, and I'm telling you she won't.

SAM

You have a lot to learn, Wayne. And you know something, the truly important lessons about life and women not in any text book. You either born with the ability to grasp them or you destined forever to be a sort of idiot, matters not how much school you go to. The question is, do you have this ability or not?

WAYNE

I hope so.

SAM

Because, if you do, I'd send you to university myself.

WAYNE

You would?

SAM

Sure I would. I've thought about it since we spoke earlier and I sure would. And let me tell you, you wouldn't have to scrunt. Living in some roach-infested dingy room, washing dishes in some stinking restaurant to help make ends meet while you should be studying your lessons. Noosiree! I'll take good care of you and all of your financial needs. I'll guide you. And somewhere along the line, I hope we'll become... well... business partners. If that happens, I'll make you more money than if you could print it yourself.

WAYNE
Why would you do this for me?

SAM
Well, in the first place, I can afford to do it. In the second place, setting up a special scholarship fund, without strings, for bright poor-people children is something I've been thinking of doing for some time. You could be the first to benefit from it, if, of course, you are deserving. But this is not the place to talk about it. Come see me at my home anytime tomorrow afternoon, let's begin to discuss your... well... glorious future. Okay? Okay ole buddy?

WAYNE
I'll be there.

(Dilys returns)

SAM
Couldn't find him?

DILYS
I found him.

SAM
You spoke to him?

DILYS
No.

(She sits by herself)

WAYNE
You'll be out here for a while, sir?

SAM

I'll be here.

WAYNE

(Indicating cassette player)

Could you continue to keep an eye on this for me please?

SAM

No problem.

WAYNE

Later.

(Wayne exits)

SAM

So what's the trouble?

DILYS

He's busy. Busy talking to that girl. They were talking intensely, as if quarrelling or something.

SAM

Yes.

DILYS

At one point she produced a handful of money and pushed it at him, but he refused it.

SAM

Money, eh?

DILYS

You think he's giving her money?

SAM

He saw you?

DILYS

I don't think so.

SAM

And you said nothing to him?

DILYS

Nothing.

(Tony enters)

TONY

I'm ready to go.

DILYS

Already? It's not even two yet.

TONY

Come on.

DILYS

I was hoping we could dance some more. One more?

TONY

It's too crowded. I don't like it when it's so crowded.
We're going home.

DILYS

Whatever you say. You want us to go, we go.

TONY

I'll get the car. Meet me up front in a minute. See you
around, Sam.

SAM

You bet. Take care, buddy.

(Tony exits)

So I guess this is where you get tucked into bed and sent off to Never-never land.

DILYS

What are you talking about?

SAM

Never mind.

DILYS

No, Sam. Tell me.

SAM

Forget it.

(Pause)

DILYS

Sam, what's the truth about the dancer girl?

SAM

You're back on that again.

DILYS

Just asking.

SAM

Why you ask?

DILYS

Call it feminine intuition. I just sense there's something there I should know.

102

SAM

There's nothing there you should know.

DILYS

I know there is, and I want to find out what it is.

SAM

If I were you, I'd leave it alone.

DILYS

I don't want to leave it alone.

SAM

Do yourself a favor, Dilys, let it rest.

DILYS

I can't let it rest till I get to the bottom of it. So be a darling and tell me who she is.

SAM

I don't want you to get hurt.

DILYS

Aha! So there is something going on to hurt me?

SAM

I didn't say that.

DILYS

Tony is in something with that girl. I know it. I just know it.

SAM

Go home, go to bed, have a good rest. Tomorrow you'll wake up and not even remember she exists.

DILYS

You may as well tell me what's going on, Sam, because I'll never stop digging until I find out the truth.

SAM

Truth can be painful.

DILYS

I want to know the truth.

SAM

Well, I'm not going to be the one to tell you.

DILYS

Sam, if the fact that we are family means anything to you, if you care about me even one little bit, you would tell me.

SAM

Tell you what. After you get home tonight, Tony is going to find some reason to leave the house. When he does, give him a headstart then jump in your car and come back here.

DILYS

For what? Why should he leave home? And why should I come back here?

SAM

Just do as I tell you. Let him leave, then come right back here.

DILYS

He's coming back here?

SAM

Come and see.

DILYS

For the girl?

SAM

Just do what I tell you and ask no more questions.

DILYS

Naah. No! I couldn't do that. I can't spy on Tony.

SAM

Good. So be it.

(Pause)

DILYS

You know, we've been married for ten years and I couldn't tell you for sure if he ever had another woman?

SAM

Really?

DILYS

I've had my suspicions, yes. People have told me things, of course. But I don't know for a fact because I have never put out myself to know and he has never flaunted any of them in my face.

SAM

And, as the saying goes, wha' eye no see heart no grieve.

DILYS

I guess.

SAM

Great. So we're right back where we started. For your own sake, take my advice and forget the whole matter. Go home with your husband, stop asking questions and continue to live in peace.

DILYS

Besides, I don't think this girl is his type anyway.

SAM

You're still dwelling on it?

DILYS

You're right. I shouldn't dwell on it. I really should just forget the whole thing.

(Silence)

Well, I mustn't keep Tony waiting. Good night, Sam. Take care of yourself.

SAM

Innocence! How I admire it, adore it, love it. But it's a virtue not suited to this life.

DILYS

Trying to tell me something, Sam?

SAM

I'm just hoping that whatever happens tonight, you will stand firm. When Tony comes up with his excuse to leave you at home alone in your nice cozy bed, promise me that whatever it takes, you will just bury your head in your pillow and go to sleep.

DILYS

I don't even think it will get to that. I have such a celebration planned for him he'll need to sleep for a week when it's over.

SAM

That's my Dilys.

(Tony enters)

TONY

All set?

DILYS

All set.

TONY

I thought you changed your mind. Come, let's get out of here.

(He leaves)

DILYS

Bye, Sam.

SAM

I'll see you soon.

DILYS

No you won't.

SAM

Good.

DILYS

You must come to Heaven more often, it's good for you. Night, night.

(She exits. Sam does a gleeful little jig, turns on the cassette player and dances. Cynthia enters. He dances towards her with his arms outstretched)

SAM

You have got to be the most fabulously sexy dancer on earth.

CYNTHIA

And you have got to be the biggest fink, the greatest crap artist and the vilest serpent on earth. Have nothing else to say to me again—ever! You hear me?

SAM

My, my, my.

CYNTHIA

And as for your $200 you can take it and stuff it for all I care.

(She flings the money at him)

SAM

You're going to explain what this is all about?

CYNTHIA

I don't have to explain nothing to you, man. Just piss off and leave me alone.

(She starts to exit)

SAM

Cynthia! Cynthia! Wait!

CYNTHIA

Wait for what?

SAM

I want to talk to you.

CYNTHIA

You can't understand English? I don't want to talk to you, ever again!

108

SAM

So you sentence and condemn me for nothing, without giving me a chance to defend myself.

CYNTHIA

For nothing? For nothing you say?

SAM

Yes! For nothing.

(He picks up money)

CYNTHIA

Roger McPherson! Think about Roger McPherson and tell me if that's for nothing.

SAM

What does Roger have to do with any of this?

CYNTHIA

I'm glad you asked. You filth, you snake, you...

SAM

Will you stop calling me names and tell me what I'm supposed to have done?

CYNTHIA

You know what you did, man. You damn well know what you did.

SAM

I don't have a clue what you're talking about.

CYNTHIA

You screwed Roger good and plenty, that's what you did.

SAM

Screwed him? I was the boy's best friend.

CYNTHIA

You made friends with him because you knew he was a pharmacist and wanted to use him.

SAM

I'm listening.

CYNTHIA

Then you got him to order all of those drugs for you. And you gave him the stamp from the hospital so the order would look official.

SAM

Who told you that?

CYNTHIA

Never mind who told me! Then when they caught up with him, you promised him if he kept his mouth shut you would make him rich for life and arrange for him to go and live in America. Then you let them send him to jail and deport him back to Guyana without one cent.

SAM

Lies! All lies.

CYNTHIA

It's true. And you damn well know it's true. Did you stop to consider his girlfriend?

SAM

I didn't even know he had a girlfriend.

CYNTHIA

His girlfriend who was pregnant? Who got kicked out of school to bring her child into the world without a father.

SAM

I had no idea about any girlfriend or any child.

CYNTHIA

Well, I am that girl.

SAM

Well, I can understand that. I understand that entirely.

CYNTHIA

You can't begin to understand it. You can't begin to understand what it is to be shunned, scorned and ridiculed by all your friends at fifteen.

(Pause)

All except by Wayne.

(Pause)

And you can't begin to understand the burden of bringing up a child by yourself. That is what you put me through.

SAM

I wasn't born with any silver spoon in my mouth, Cynthia. I know from bitter first-hand experience how tough life is. So believe me, I understand. But the truth is, you accusing me of doing things I never did.

111

CYNTHIA

Don't give me that, man. Roger told me all about it himself. The only thing he wouldn't tell me was who set him up, for fear of what they would do him, or worse yet do me and the child. But I found out to-night who did it. You, Samuel Drummonds! You and nobody else but you, so don't come telling me no nonsense.

SAM

Okay, let's back up a bit. Why you giving me back the money?

CYNTHIA

I don't need you or your blood money, man. Just leave me alone and go to hell.

SAM

Surely the smart thing to do is pocket the money and still tell me go to hell.

CYNTHIA

The smart thing for you to do.

SAM

For anybody to do. And you seem like a smart girl to me. So giving me back the money doesn't make sense.

CYNTHIA

My boyfriend does not want me to keep your money. And I do not want to keep your filthy money either.

SAM

Aha! Now I get it. But you're really not so smart after all. I give you something, that's between me and you. You had no call running to your boyfriend blabbing off your mouth about it.

CYNTHIA

Me, blabbing off my mouth? Don't make me laugh! Don't make me laugh! You're the one who ran to tell him, bragging off about what and what not you're going to do with me for a lousy 200 bucks. As if 200 bucks is money.

SAM

Where's your senses? You think I'd say such a thing to your boyfriend?

CYNTHIA

You didn't' know he's my boyfriend.

SAM

Who doesn't know he's your boyfriend?

CYNTHIA

You didn't! You hardly knew I even existed until tonight.

SAM

Tony is my lawyer and my personal friend. I have to know who his girlfriend is.

CYNTHIA

If he's such a good friend, then why you trying to pick me up in the first place?

(Wayne enters)

WAYNE

Hey, Cynthia, standing by?

CYNTHIA

For what?

113

WAYNE

For when they call the winners, dumb, dumb.

CYNTHIA

Oh, yes, of course.

WAYNE

You'll be here?

CYNTHIA

Yes, I'll be here.

WAYNE

Cool. I'll come and get you.

CYNTHIA

Hey, Wayne, you want to hear something? Is this son-of-a-bitch you see here made them deport Roger, you know.

WAYNE

Mr. Drummonds?

CYNTHIA

What the hell Mr. Drummonds? This scumbag here that you look up to and respect is worse than a snake. Nobody dealing more drugs than him, you know.

WAYNE

No, man, Cyn. Not Mr. Drummonds.

CYNTHIA

Think, Wayne. How else could he get all this money he throwing 'round? You think his stupid little shop could make all that money?

114

SAM

Stupid little shop? Don't be ridiculous. Would you call my store a stupid little shop, Wayne? And in any case, what would she, or anyone else for that matter, know about what my shop makes or doesn't make? What could she know about my many investments and other sources of income?

CYNTHIA

I know you dealing drugs. You know you dealing drugs, and anybody else who want to know only have to open their own two eyes and see.

SAM

Utter nonsense.

CYNTHIA

You dealing drugs! He's a stinking, nasty, dirty drug dealer, Wayne, and you could tell de world me, Cynthia Corbett, tell you so.

WAYNE

Look, come with me. Come let's go inside.

CYNTHIA

And you want to hear something else? I just gee him back his $200. Ley him tek it and stuff it.

WAYNE

Come let's go dance.

CYNTHIA

No, man, me no finish with him yet.

WAYNE

No, Cynthia. Come with me.

CYNTHIA

Me safe, Wayne.

SAM

You're right, Wayne, go dance with her.

CYNTHIA

Stinking, dutty, drugs dealer! How they let you in here, eh? How they let you loose among decent people?

WAYNE

Come, let's go, Cynthia.

CYNTHIA

Me a'right, Wayne, believe me.

WAYNE

You believe he did what you said to Roger?

CYNTHIA

He did it yes.

WAYNE

You believe he dealing drugs?

CYNTHIA

Of course, he dealing drugs. Stinking, dutty drugs dealer. Murderer!

WAYNE

Then what you want to be out here with him for? Why you even want to be in his company?

CYNTHIA

Me no done tell him all I have to say yet, man.

116

SAM

Well, I'm through listening to your damn nonsense. Pay no attention to rubbish and idle gossip, Wayne. You're a smart boy. Smart enough, I think, to see for yourself. So come by my home tomorrow afternoon as planned and see for yourself.

CYNTHIA

You going by his house tomorrow?

WAYNE

Well, he invited me, yes.

CYNTHIA

Don't go, Wayne. If you don't want what happen to Roger to happen to you, don't go.

SAM

More rubbish and idle gossip.

CYNTHIA

Don't go, Wayne, don't ever let this evil snake get close to you.

SAM

Well, Wayne, you can choose to listen to this rubbish or to see about your future. It's a matter entirely up to you.

(Tony enters)

TONY

Still trying to steal my girl, eh, Sam?

SAM

Well, to be perfectly honestly with you, yes, but she's a bit too much for me.

CYNTHIA

You better believe that.

WAYNE

Look, you coming with me?

CYNTHIA

It's alright now, man. Everything safe now. Come back for me when it's time. Alright?

(Wayne withdraws)

TONY

Too much for you, eh?

SAM

That's right. She's all yours.

TONY

I should hope so. But, don't give up. Plenty angels in Heaven tonight. You could try your luck inside.

SAM

No thanks. There's only one angel for me and you have her already.

CYNTHIA

Two's company and three's a crowd.

SAM

Trying to tell me something, dear?

CYNTHIA

Yes. Get lost.

SAM

My, my, well, guess I might as well.

(He heads for the exit)

Anything I can get you love birds from inside?

TONY

Nothing at all.

SAM

Take care then.

TONY

See you around, Sam.

SAM

Night, Angel.

CYNTHIA

Piss off. Creep.

(Sam exits)

TONY

God, you got a dirty mouth.

CYNTHIA

Kiss it and make it clean.

(They kiss)

Thanks for coming back.

TONY

Anything for you, sweetheart. You know that.

CYNTHIA

Boy you should have heard me giving it to your friend, Sam Drummonds. I took him apart and threw his $200 back on him.

TONY

Good.

CYNTHIA

You should have seen me.

TONY

You didn't have to lie to me about the $200, though.

CYNTHIA

Is only because you're so touchy about these things, hon.

TONY

I don't take good enough care of you?

CYNTHIA

You know it's not that, darling.

TONY

So what is it then? Just an easy 200 bucks you couldn't pass up?

CYNTHIA

That's what you think it is?

TONY

I want you to tell me what it is.

CYNTHIA

I didn't ask him for the money, Tony. He gave it to me. He gave it to me in an envelope, so I didn't even know what it was.

TONY

You lied to me and I don't like that.

CYNTHIA

And you, of course, always tell me the truth.

TONY

You lied to me! Lied!

CYNTHIA

Oh, for Christ sake, man, if this is what you came back here for you may as well go back home to your stupid wife.

(Pause)

TONY

Okay. If that's what you want, no problem with me.

(He starts to exit)

CYNTHIA

Go ahead! Go right ahead for all I care.

(He leaves and she sits by herself waiting. Shortly he returns and stands up stage watching her)

TONY

You're a real bitch, you know that?

CYNTHIA

Oh, darling, don't say that. Don't even think it.

(She embraces him)

TONY

You had no right to lie to me.

CYNTHIA

You know how you are, Tony. You would have over reacted. You would have made a mountain out of a molehill, just as you're doing now.

TONY

I would have done no such thing.

121

CYNTHIA

Sure you would. You would have wanted to know
what I did, what I said to him, how I looked at him,
to give him the impression that I'm available for
$200?

TONY

Well, now that you mention it, what did you do?
What did you say to him? How did you look at him to
give him the impression that you are available?

CYNTHIA

God! You see what I mean?

TONY

You see? You don't even know when I'm joking.
Come here.

(Cynthia walks to Tony looking at him quizzically. He
kisses her and her arms come up around his neck.
Dilys enters. She sees what is happening, but doesn't
want so see; doesn't want to believe)

DILYS

(To herself)

No! Oh, God, no, no, no!

(She retreats to the shadows)

CYNTHIA

Am I forgiven?

TONY

Not yet. You have to do some more penance first.

CYNTHIA

Goodie. Let's go dance.

TONY

Let's cut out from here instead.

CYNTHIA

But I want to wait until they announce the winners of the contest. Please? It should be any minute now and then we can leave right after that, okay?

TONY

(Resignedly)

Whatever you say, I'm all yours.

CYNTHIA

No wonder I love you so much.

(They kiss passionately)

I'll go hurry them up.

TONY

Do that.

(Cynthia starts to run off)

And Cynthia, make it quick.

CYNTHIA

Naughty boy.

(She exits. He chuckles. Long pause during which Dilys comes out of the shadows)

DILYS

Tony.

TONY

Hey... Dilys? What the... what you doing back here?

DILYS

How could you Tony? How could you, man?

TONY

What you talking about?

DILYS

How could you humiliate me like this? How could you?

TONY

Dilys... look... I don't have a clue what you're talking about.

DILYS

This is the urgent call you had to make to London? That you had to make tonight because London is five hours ahead and you had to catch your client before he flew to New York? That you had to make from your office because you didn't have the number at home? This is it? Oh, God no.

(She cries)

TONY

Come on, Dilys, get a hold of yourself.

DILYS

How long you been feeding me this kind of crap, Tony?

TONY

Dilys... Dilys...

DILYS

How long?

TONY

Listen, Dilys. Let me explain it to you.

DILYS

Go ahead and explain it.

TONY

Well... you see...

DILYS

I don't see.

(Cynthia returns)

TONY

Look, Dilys...

DILYS

Explain how you could dump me on our anniversary night to be in the arms of—this!

CYNTHIA

This what?

DILYS

This slut here. Yes! This little slut.

CYNTHIA

Look, who de hell you calling a slut you stupid old cow? Who you...

TONY

Cynthia! Shut up!

DILYS

Come on, Tony we're going home.

(She takes his arm)

CYNTHIA

(Taking the other arm)

You not going any place, Tony. You staying right here.

DILYS

Come ahead, Tony.

CYNTHIA

I say you staying right here.

TONY

Please... please...

DILYS

Let go my husband.

CYNTHIA

Leggo me man.

TONY

Would the two of you let go of me.

DILYS

I say you're coming home with me now.

CYNTHIA

I say he staying right here with me.

DILYS

(Releasing him)

Listen, I'm not going to be in any tug of war for you. Forget that.

CYNTHIA

Good. Now get lost.

DILYS

You going to stand there and let her talk to me like that?

TONY

Listen, Dilys, the best place for us to deal with this matter is at home. Let me join you there shortly and we can talk it over then.

DILYS

I don't believe this. I really don't believe I'm hearing you right.

CYNTHIA

Let her go about her damn business and wait till you come home, Tony. Is jail she have you in jail?

DILYS

Make up your mind, Tony, and make it up now. It's either me or—this.

CYNTHIA

Go 'way. You can't see when you not welcome?

DILYS

Either you come with me now and let's try and find a way to patch this mess up, or stay here and come home to an empty house.

TONY

Don't talk nonsense.

DILYS

You may think it's nonsense. Well, don't come with me now, and I promise you on my mother's grave, when you do get home I and our three children will be gone. And the next time you hear from me will be through my lawyer asking for a divorce. So make your choice.

TONY

I'll meet you at home in a minute.

DILYS

No. That's not good enough.

TONY

Well, it better be good enough.

DILYS

Well, I'm telling you, Mr. Thompson, that it's not good enough! It could never be good enough.

TONY

So what's good enough, then?

DILYS

That you come with me now. That we leave here together as husband and wife.

CYNTHIA

Don't even listen to her, eh, Tony.

DILYS

I will not have you humiliate me further, Tony. I deserve better than that. I demand better than that. So make up your mind and make it up now.

TONY

Come on. Let's go.

(Sam enters)

CYNTHIA

(To Tony)

You son of a bitch. You awful son of a bitch.

TONY

Hey, she's my wife. What the hell you expect me to do?

(Cynthia rushes off to open field)

SAM

Well spoken.

(To Dilys)

What you doing back here?

DILYS

I came to get my husband, that's all.

(She exits)

SAM

How's my tough buddy doing?

TONY

Sam Drummonds. Yep. I can smell your hand in this.

SAM

In what?

TONY

You put Dilys up to this, you son of a bitch!

SAM

Me? Surprise at you. I wouldn't know how to play that rough.

TONY

I ought to break your frigging neck.

SAM

Easy, Tony, take it easy. You don't want to do anything to embarrass your wife.

TONY

I'm warning you, Sam, stay away from her.

SAM

Look, if it will make you feel any better. I'll stay away from her. For the sake of our friendship I'll stay away from her. And I'll tell you why. Perspective. Perspective and priorities. I happen to believe it's better in all ways for us to be friends than to be at war. And I can see the girl is special to you. So in the best interest of business and friendship I'm going to back off and leave your girl alone. Better than that, I'm going to leave now, with you, and go home. How's that?

TONY

(He doesn't respond but moves towards field where Cynthia is)

Cynthia. Cynthia! Be cool.

CYNTHIA

Piss off!

SAM

Let's not keep Dilys waiting.

(They start moving off)

Perspective is what's important, Tony. Perspective and priorities. Let's not lose sight of them and send our world up in smoke over nonsense.

(They both exit. Presently, Wayne enters in a state of excitement)

WAYNE

Cynthia! Cynthia!

(Pause)

Cyn?

CYNTHIA

(Coming back on stage)

Do not call me Cyn!

WAYNE

Come on. Come on, Cynthia, everybody calling for you! We won! You hear me? We won the contest!

(Pause)

Hey, what's wrong?

CYNTHIA

Nothing.

WAYNE

Well come, let's go. De whole place clamoring for you.

CYNTHIA

You go.

WAYNE

Without you?

CYNTHIA

Tell them I gone home.

WAYNE

No, man. It wouldn't be de same without you.

CYNTHIA

Just go ahead alone no man.

WAYNE

What's wrong? Something happen between you and Tony?

CYNTHIA

I just wish de world would open and swallow me.

WAYNE

What he did you?

CYNTHIA

He hurt me, man. He hurt me bad.

WAYNE

He hit you?

CYNTHIA

No.

WAYNE

You never listen to me, do you?

CYNTHIA

Ah wonder if he think I'm goin' let him get way with it?

WAYNE

What he did you?

CYNTHIA

Ah wonder if he really think so?

WAYNE

Let's go get our first prize. It will make you feel better.

CYNTHIA

Ah goin' find a way to hurt him back.

WAYNE

Just forget him.

CYNTHIA

Ah goin' hurt him so bad, he will wish he never once messed with me.

WAYNE

What you goin' do? Look, Cynthia, just forget him. Forget him as you should have done from day one. As you should have done before you ever got involved with him. Put him out of your life and keep him out.

CYNTHIA

Put him out and keep him out, yes. But ah goin' hurt him too.

(Sam enters)

SAM

Look, they're getting on crazy for the two of you in there.

WAYNE

Come on, Cynthia, let's go.

CYNTHIA

Ah really can't face anybody now.

WAYNE

You could handle it, man.

CYNTHIA

No. Go without me, Wayne, please.

WAYNE

Okay, see you later then.

(He rushes off. Presently Sam enters)

SAM

I brought you a rum and coke.

(Pause)

You look like you need it.

CYNTHIA

You damn right.

(She drinks all of it)

SAM

I also have something else that belongs to you.

CYNTHIA

What's that?

134

SAM

(Producing the $200)

This. Take it and buy yourself something nice to celebrate.

CYNTHIA

(Taking the money)

I see.

SAM

And, if there's anything I could ever do to help, anything, don't hesitate to call. Enjoy the rest of the
night.

(He starts to exit)

CYNTHIA

Er… Mr. Drummonds…

SAM

Sam.

CYNTHIA

Sam. Is your wine nicely chilled?

SAM

The white is perfectly chilled. Red is at room tempera-
ture, as it should be.

CYNTHIA

And how's the music?

SAM

Anything you want from Arrow to Tchaikovsky.

CYNTHIA

And what's for breakfast?

SAM

Name it and you will have it.

(He tries to embrace her but she doesn't let him)

CYNTHIA

There's only one problem. I don't want to be coaxed, or forced, or tricked into anything.

SAM

Absolutely.

CYNTHIA

If you can accept those terms I'll be your guest for the night, what's left of it.

SAM

I'll tell you what, you can have it whatever way you want. If everything is not to your liking you could leave tomorrow and never come back again. If you like, and so desire, you can let my house be your house. Come whenever you like.

CYNTHIA

We'll see.

SAM

Well, I'm ready whenever you are.

(Wayne enters)

WAYNE

(To Cynthia)

You okay?

CYNTHIA

Yeah, I guess.

SAM

She couldn't be better. And congratulations.

WAYNE

Thank you.

(To Cynthia)

Here's your half of the prize money.

CYNTHIA

Keep it.

WAYNE

No way. You earned it, you keep it.

CYNTHIA

I'm giving it to you, dumb, dumb.

WAYNE

Well, I'm through accepting charity tonight.

CYNTHIA

My contribution to your last year of school. A sort of loan. If you don't pass all your subjects you pay me back. Hell, no. You doan pass, I come hounding you for my 100 bucks.

WAYNE

Consider your money dead.

SAM

I'll get the car.

CYNTHIA

Okay.

(Sam exits)

WAYNE

Car? Wha' car. Wha' he mean he going for the car?

CYNTHIA

What you think?

WAYNE

You going with him?

CYNTHIA

He taking me home, Wayne.

WAYNE

To your home?

CYNTHIA

You have to ask?

WAYNE

Yes.

CYNTHIA

Well... actually... no. To his home.

WAYNE

You not serious.

CYNTHIA

I am.

WAYNE

Don't do it, Cynthia.

CYNTHIA

Why?

WAYNE

Because... well...

CYNTHIA

And please don't tell me to protect my good name, or my virtue, or because it don't look good, or any of that crap.

WAYNE

Alright I wouldn't tell you that. I'm just asking you not to do it.

CYNTHIA

For you, right?

WAYNE

Yes, for me.

CYNTHIA

Well, you out of luck. I'm through doing things for you tonight.

WAYNE

Do it because he's a stinking, duttty, drugs dealer and he can't be good for you.

CYNTHIA

My mind done mek up an' me nar change it.

WAYNE

Those are your own words, Cynthia: A stinking, dutty drugs dealer.

CYNTHIA

I'm going home with him, Wayne.

WAYNE

Murderer!

CYNTHIA

I'm not listening to you.

WAYNE

Murderer!

(Pause)

CYNTHIA

You still going to see him tomorrow?

WAYNE

Why?

CYNTHIA

Just asking.

WAYNE

So you can be gone by the time I get there? Or so you can be all set to entertain me, as mistress of the manor?

CYNTHIA

For chrissake, man, is just a simple question! What he want you to come to his house for, anyway? What he promise you?

WAYNE

Well, he promise to send me to med-school—in grand style. He wants to guide me and hopes we will become business partners. And... er... if this happens he promise he would make me more money than if I had a press to print it myself.

CYNTHIA

Tempted?

WAYNE

Of course I'm tempted.

CYNTHIA

And?

WAYNE

What you think?

CYNTHIA

You have to decide.

WAYNE

No, no. Tell me what you think I should do.

CYNTHIA

I can't decide for you, Wayne.

WAYNE

I'm not asking you to decide for me. I'm asking what you want me to do.

CYNTHIA

Well, don't ask me that.

WAYNE

You want what happen to Roger, or worse, to happen to me? Is that what you want, Cynthia?

CYNTHIA

Look! Do whatever you think is best for you. I'm looking out for myself. That's what I'm doing, for a change.

(Pause)

141

CYNTHIA (Continued)

I've been used, abused, and manipulated...

WAYNE

And you just setting up yourself to be used, abused, and manipulated all over again.

CYNTHIA

No, not again. Not this time around. This time I'm looking out for me.

WAYNE

Looking out for you how?

CYNTHIA

Me Cynthia Corbett. Some kind of happiness must be out there for me too. All I want is a little bit of happiness.

WAYNE

With Sam Drummonds?

CYNTHIA

With whoever. My luck with him can't get any worse.

WAYNE

What happen with you and Tony tonight?

CYNTHIA

Don't even call his name to me, okay? Just tell yourself that over and done with. This is a new Cynthia you talking to and my new motto is do unto others before they do unto me. That's my key to happiness.

WAYNE

You doan listen to me enough, Cynthia.

CYNTHIA

And am not listening to your objections to this either. Come, I'll let Sam give you a ride home.

WAYNE

Thanks, but no thanks.

CYNTHIA

It's late. You going have a hard time getting a ride now.

WAYNE

I'll make my own way.

CYNTHIA

It's too far.

WAYNE

I'll make my own way.

CYNTHIA

As you wish.

(She exits. Wayne turns on his tape recorder. A mournful tune is heard and he starts to work out a choreography. Cynthia returns and watches for a while)

CYNTHIA

All four of Sam's tires are slashed. You wouldn't know anything about that would you?

WAYNE

Moi?

CYNTHIA

Yes, you, Wayne Cabey.

(He continues to dance. Cynthia takes off the music)

I'm talking to you, man. Did you cut de man tires?

WAYNE

You never listen to me. And I couldn't very well let him take you home now, could I?

CYNTHIA

How you know he was goin' take me home?

WAYNE

He told me. He said he understands people and he was one hundred percent certain he would take you home tonight.

CYNTHIA

He did?

WAYNE

I said no way. He said wait and see. He said I was young and innocent. That I still had a lot to learn about human nature and about women in particular. So just in case he was right I had to make it hard for him.

CYNTHIA

What's to stop me from going with him still?

WAYNE

I doan know, but I'll find something. I just hope you come to your senses before I have to start getting drastic.

CYNTHIA

He's not stupid, he's going to know who cut his tires.

144

WAYNE

Big deal.

CYNTHIA

And what about med-school?

WAYNE

I'll get to med-school.

CYNTHIA

All four tires. You'll do anything to stop me going home with Sam?

WAYNE

Just about anything, yes. I love you and I just don't want to see you getting messed up with Sam Drummonds.

(Long pause)

CYNTHIA

You always look out for me, don't you. You're the only man I know who always look out for me, just for me. And still sometimes I treat you like dirt.

WAYNE

You just don't listen to me enough, that's all.

CYNTHIA

Well, I'm going to have to start changing that.

WAYNE

Do that. And whatever else you do, don't go getting sentimental on me now. Okay? Come check this out.

(He switches back on the music)

145

CYNTHIA

You have a part for me?

WAYNE

Sure. Listen, feel it, and join in when you're ready.

(She joins him and they dance together, growing more and more into it and loosing themselves in the dance. Sam enters and watches. He applauds wildly)

SAM

Fantastic!

WAYNE

You like it, Sam?

SAM

Out of this world.

(To Cynthia)

Ready? I managed to get a taxi. He's waiting for us.

CYNTHIA

I changed my mind, Sam. I'm staying with Wayne.

SAM

Oh. Why don't you both come along?

WAYNE

Thanks, but no thanks.

SAM

Really, it would be no problem at all.

WAYNE

No problem for you, maybe, but a definite problem for me. You see, Sam, Sam Drummonds, I'm simply not going your way. And just in case you still hoping to send me to school, let me tell you as plain as I could. I'm not going to be involved with you. Not now, not ever. Not even if it would make me the richest man on earth. Not even if it's the only chance I have of making it through med school.

SAM

You're a damn arse. That's all you are. And I suspect that's all you'll ever be.

WAYNE

I sure hope you're right.

SAM

Sure you don't want to come with me, Cynthia?

CYNTHIA

Quite sure.

SAM

Well, you know how to find me. Call any time. I'll be waiting.

CYNTHIA

Don't hold your breath.

SAM

Oh, you'll come, pretty little girl. Take my word for it, sooner or later you'll come. In the meantime, Wayne, try and take care of her—as best you can.

(He starts to exit)

SAM (Continued)

By the way, Wayne, you wouldn't happen to know how all four of my tires managed to get slashed tonight?

WAYNE

I have a pretty good idea.

SAM

Thought you would.

WAYNE

Some man who intends to put a spoke in your wheel, who intends to slow you down, took a big knife and cut your tires.

SAM

(Laughing)

Well, what the hell, maybe there's hope for you yet. Maybe there is. Look, call me sometime. Better yet, drop by and see me. Both of you.

(He exits)

CYNTHIA

My God, Wayne, all four of the man tires? Two woulda been more than enough, you devil.

(They embrace warmly. He lifts and spins her)

WAYNE

Want to take it from the top again?

CYNTHIA

You doan see is morning?

WAYNE

No better time.

CYNTHIA

For real. Yeah, for real.

(He fidgets with the tape recorder. The music comes up and they dance tenderly as the lights slowly fade to black)

THE END